Gappy's Great Escape

Also by Star Donovan

A Surprise for Gappy

Gappy Disappears

Gappy is Kidnapped

Gappy and the Thieves

Gappy's Great Escape

Book Five of
The Young Vampire Adventures
by
Star Donovan

Illustrations and cover art
by
Ann-Cathrine Loo

Bronwynn Press

Published by
Bronwynn Press, LLC
PO Box 297
Troy, NY 12182

First edition, 2010
Library of Congress Control Number: 2010939115
ISBN-13: 978-0-9821404-8-2
ISBN-10: 0-9821404-8-7

Bronwynn Press

Contents

Prologue

In the darkness of the night down by the train tracks, a gust of wind picked up some tattered sheets of newspaper and blew them along the ground. They came to rest next to a metal barrel of burning garbage that had been lit with a match ten minutes previously. A dirty hand reached down, picked up the newspapers, and added them to the greedily-devouring flames.

The hand belonged to a thin man who lived in a cardboard box nearby. Thin brown hair straggled over the collar of his old, ripped jacket that was much too big for him, and wisps of hair straggled from his chin. The face above the chin was grey with dirt and weariness from years of struggling to survive. He had almost forgotten his name, but people at the shelter, where he stayed in the winter months, had nicknamed him Cobbler because he used to be a shoemaker long ago.

The man's stomach rumbled as he dug into the pocket of his baggy jeans. He took out a piece of dried bread and examined it with a sigh. It was going to be another hungry night. As he began to nibble the hard crust, a gold tooth in the front of his mouth glinted in the glow of the flickering flames.

Suddenly a black panel van appeared at the end of the street and drove up to him. The homeless man watched curiously as it stopped nearby and a classy-looking couple got out – a gentleman wearing a long, dark coat and a woman dressed in tight, black pants and sweater, a pair of pointy, high-heeled boots on her feet. Cobbler wondered if they were lost and cleared his throat raspily, expecting them to ask him for directions. They certainly looked out of place – especially the woman. She picked her way across the rough ground, looking around her with a sneer on her face as if she smelled something nasty. She probably did. The homeless man had not had a bath in weeks.

When they reached the metal barrel, the gentleman held his hands over the warmth of the flames while the woman ran her eyes over the bedraggled Cobbler from head to toe, her white face glowing in the darkness. She nodded to her companion.

"Needs some work, but he'll do. Take him."

"Wha–?" Cobbler protested as the gentleman in the long coat came around the barrel and grabbed his shoulders. The homeless man struggled, but it was no use. His captor was immensely strong, with a grip of iron. He hustled poor Cobbler toward the van, opened the rear door, picked him up, and shoved him in.

As Cobbler landed on an old mattress lying on the floor of the van, all of his fear and anxiety suddenly left him, and a strange calmness overtook his body. He lay back on the mattress and gazed up at his captors, not caring what happened next. As his limbs became heavy, his fingers released the piece of bread he had been holding in his hand. The woman picked it up with a thumb and forefinger, a look of distaste on her face, and threw it over her shoulder as the man with the iron grip closed the door and locked it.

Cobbler did not hear the front doors slam, nor did he feel the lurch as they left the curb. He was already asleep as the van drove away, leaving behind it the remnants of his life – a glowing garbage barrel, a cardboard box, and a piece of bread.

Chapter One

A New Vampire Power

Gustavus Grapple sat hunched on a chair in his bedroom, staring at a toy car that stood on the desk in front of him. He had been sitting that way for almost twenty minutes, and his neck was getting stiff, but he was concentrating very hard. At any moment that car was going to move by itself.

"Stupid hair!" he exclaimed suddenly as a long lock of his black hair flopped down over one eye. "I almost had it."

He stood up and stretched, then sat down to try again. With a little frown on his pale forehead, he forced himself to think of nothing but the image of his left hand reaching out to touch the car. After about a minute, his eyes dry from not blinking, his chest full to bursting from holding his breath, he began to almost see a very faint, ghostly outline of his left hand reaching . . . reaching . . . r-e-a-c-h –

"Gappy," his mother yelled up the stairs.

The kids at school had first nicknamed him Gappy when he had lost his top two front teeth in second grade and started driving people crazy by whistling through the gap. Goodness knows why his parents, Cuthbert and Livinia Grapple, had chosen the name Gustavus. Gappy liked his nickname better, except when the school bullies called him Crappy Gappy.

"Dinner's getting cold," Mom yelled again.

Gappy got up from his chair with a sigh. Just a few more seconds, and that car would have moved. He was sure of it.

"Why do you look so miserable?" asked Dad as his son came into the kitchen. "Bad day at school?"

Gappy sat down at the table where his mother was setting out plates of warthog liver and bacon with sweet-potato fries. He grabbed the ketchup. "I was trying to do telekinesis."

"Telekinesis?" questioned Mom, frowning at the amount of ketchup Gappy was pouring over his warthog liver.

"Yeah, you know? Moving things with your mind," Gappy said.

"I know what it is," said Mom, "but why did you suddenly decide to try it?"

Gappy closed the cap of the ketchup bottle. "It's a vampire power, isn't it? I saw it in a movie."

"Yes, it is," said Dad, wrinkling his sandy moustache, "but you're way too young to learn it yet, Gappy. Vampires don't develop that skill until they're older."

"Way older," Mom put in.

"Well, I read about it on the Internet," said Gappy. "You have to meditate first to clear your mind, then focus on the object you're trying to move. I've been staring at a toy car for about twenty minutes without blinking, and I was just starting to feel like it was going to move any second, when you ruined it by calling me down for dinner."

Mom laughed. "Well, sorry. You can try again later, but don't expect it to work."

Gappy made a face and did not answer. The telekinesis was going to work. It *was!*

Dad saw his expression and patted his shoulder. "Eat up, Gappy. You need to keep your strength up if you're going to be moving things with your mind."

After dinner, knowing that Gappy was eager to continue his experiment, Mom excused him from dish duty and sent him upstairs with a glass of purple rattlesnake juice.

Gappy sat down at his desk again and closed his eyes for a moment to focus on clearing his mind. Then he sat on his hands, hunched over with his chin almost touching the top of the desk, and stared at the toy car. This time the image of his ghostly hand appeared in his mind's eye much quicker than before, and soon he was back to the stage he had reached earlier before being interrupted.

As he stared and stared, his imaginary hand moved closer . . . closer . . .

. . . and one fingertip touched the car!

Heart pumping with excitement, Gappy forced himself to hold his breath just a few seconds longer, summoned up his will, and . . .

. . . gave the car a little nudge!

With eyes as dry as sand, his head swimming from lack of oxygen, Gappy stared in amazement as the car trembled and then moved half an inch to the right.

"Phooooooh!" The breath exploded out of him and he gulped in air, rapidly blinking his gritty eyes.

"I did it! I did it!" he yelped, but softly. He did not want Mom and Dad to know until he had tried it again to be sure he had not imagined it. Even now as he looked at the car, could he honestly tell that it had moved at all? Maybe the lack of oxygen had made his eyes wobble.

No, he had to make sure.

Gappy stuck a piece of Scotch tape on the desk and placed the car with its back wheels just touching the right edge of it so that he would be able to tell if it moved. Then he took some slow, deep breaths in and out and tried to calm the excitement that was fluttering around in his brain. After a few seconds he felt ready. Keeping his breathing slow and steady, he closed his eyes and cleared his mind, then sat on his hands, leaned forward, and stared at the car.

Soon the ghostly image of his hand appeared in his mind's eye. It did not hesitate this time but smoothly reached out, lifted a finger, and gave the car a sharp push. Gappy's eyes had not even started to dry out yet, nor was he out of breath, but this time there was definitely no doubt that the car was moving. It shot sideways off the desk and landed on the floor!

Gappy jumped up from his chair. "I did it! I did it!" he yelled at the top of his voice. He flung open his bedroom door and hurtled down the stairs. "Mom! Dad! I did it! I did it! I can do telekinesis!"

His parents dashed out of the living room. "What?" Dad exclaimed.

"You did?" Mom yelled at the same time.

"Yeah!" Gappy panted, jumping up and down in his excitement. He grabbed his parents' hands. "I moved the car! Come look!"

He did not have to drag them up the stairs. They were excited too. Could their vampire son really do telekinesis, at only ten years old?

They all crowded into Gappy's bedroom. Gappy picked up the toy car and set it down on the tape on his desk. Then he flung himself down on his chair, clutched the sides of the seat with both hands, and closed his eyes.

Mom and Dad stood silently as Gappy slowly took a few deep breaths then opened his eyes and stared at the toy car. After a few seconds, the car wobbled slightly and . . . shot off the desk again!

Mom shrieked, and Dad just stood with his mouth open wide in surprise.

Gappy turned to them, a huge grin on his face. "See? I told you I could do it. Isn't it awesome?"

His amazed parents looked at each another. "Can you believe it, Livvie?" Dad asked.

Mom shook her head. "No. He's too young. What does this mean, Burt? Is he going to be like his great-great-grandfather,

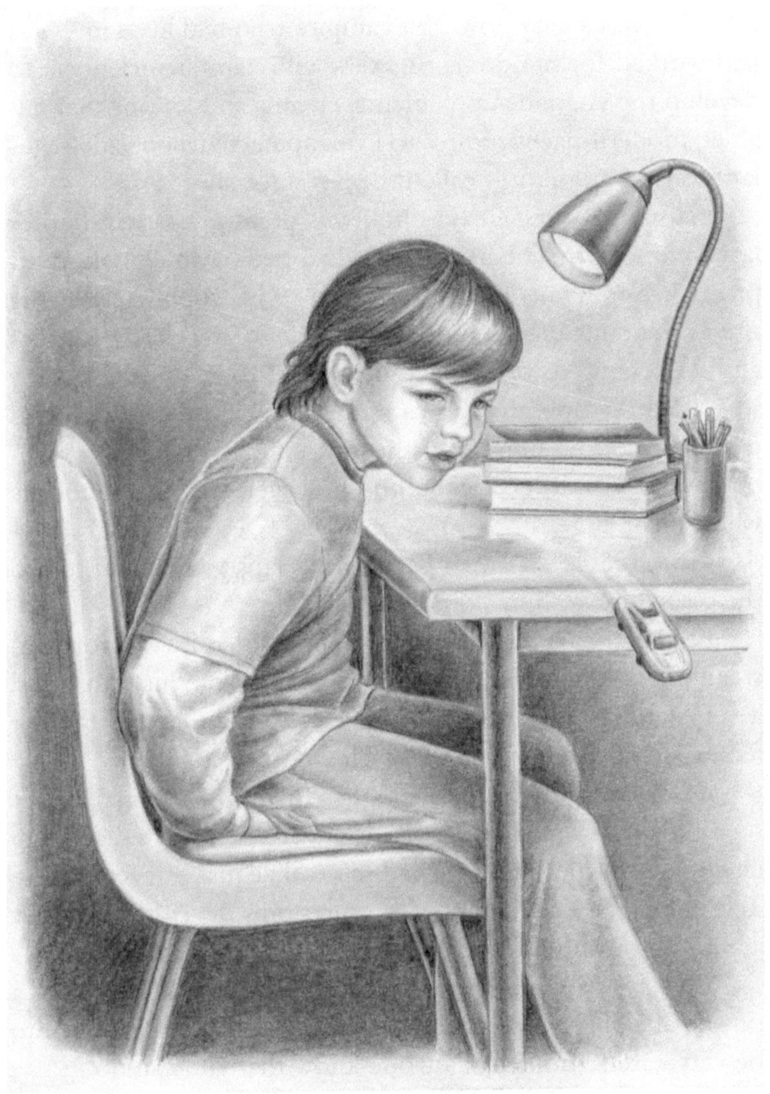

It shot sideways off the desk.

do you think?"

"Wow, you mean Tristan Glyndwr?" asked Gappy. Tristan Glyndwr was a very powerful vampire who had lived in Wales and worked for hundreds of years with vampire scientists to develop the vitamin supplements, creams and lotions that enabled modern-day vampires to live undetected alongside regular humans – vampires called them *regs* for short.

Gappy had first heard about his great-great-grandfather last summer when he had been kidnapped by an evil old vampire, Charles Artois Durante, known to his supporters as the *Master*. Durante despised the New Order of modern vampires and was trying to bring back the Old Order. Luckily Gappy was able to escape, and the Vampire Council had captured Durante and locked him up in the Brookmore Prison for Vampires. He was still very dangerous, however, and his supporters were still at large.

Mr. Grapple sat down heavily on Gappy's bed and patted the place next to him. "Sit down, son."

Feeling a little apprehensive, Gappy did as he was told. Instead of looking excited and happy for his son, his father had a very serious expression on his face. So did Gappy's mother as she sat down on the bed as well.

"What is it?" Gappy asked. "Is something wrong?"

"Not really," said Dad. "I know you're all excited at being able to do telekinesis, but you don't realize just how big this is. Telekinesis is a skill that most vampires only develop when they are in their twenties. You're only just under eleven years old."

"Yes, it's very rare for a vampire your age to master such a powerful skill," Mom added, looking worried. "We'll have to be very careful not to let anyone know that you can do it."

"I agree," said Dad. "If the wrong people found out, they'd be dying to get their hands on you to make you use your powers for some evil purpose."

Mom nodded. "Yes. There was a case a few years ago. A fourteen-year-old vampire in England was kidnapped by a bunch of evil vampires who were trying to break into the Tower of London to steal the Crown Jewels. He was another wonder child whose specialty was walking through metal. It didn't matter how thick it was – he could *particalize* through it, easy as anything."

"Wow," said Gappy. "You have to be really good to do that. I've only been able to walk through bricks and rock, so far."

"So you can see why we have to be careful, Gappy," said Mom earnestly, taking her son's hand in hers. "There are so many opportunities out there for rogue vampires to use their powers for criminal activity."

"We must inform the Vampire Council about your new skill, of course," said Dad, "but that's as far as it goes, Gappy. Do you understand?"

Gappy sighed. "I can't even tell Pru?" Prudence Pottage was his best friend and one of the few regular humans who knew that Gappy and his parents were vampires.

Mr. Grapple shook his head. "No. If Pru knew, she could also be in danger. We have to keep this to ourselves."

Gappy pouted. His whole world had been turned upside down when he was nine years old and had first learned from his parents that he was turning into a vampire. Ever since then he had had to be very careful not to reveal his secret identity to regular humans. Now here was another secret that he had to hide from other vampires as well.

"Oh, man! I was so excited about being able to move things with my mind, and now I can't even tell my best friend. That stinks!"

Mom laughed as she pushed herself up from Gappy's bed. "Well, Dad and I are both excited for you, dear. It's a huge accomplishment and quite amazing to see our son apparently following in his great-great-grandfather's footsteps."

"I never asked you this before," said Gappy, "but whatever happened to Grandpa Glyndwr?"

His mother froze and glanced at her husband.

Dad took off his tortoiseshell glasses and rubbed his eyes. "No one knows, Gappy. He disappeared a hundred years ago."

"What!" Gappy exclaimed, puzzled. "What do you mean disappeared? You mean he could still be alive? I thought he was dead."

Mom bent to pick up the toy car from the floor, her long, straight hair falling across her face like a glossy, black curtain. She held the car for a moment, turning it over and over in her slender hands, then set it down on the desk. She turned a sad face to Gappy and shrugged.

"We don't know. He came over to the States to work with some vampire scientists who were building a new factory for making our vitamins. One day he just didn't show up for work. The Council organized a worldwide search, but he was never seen again. It's almost as if he disappeared into thin air. I was so sad. I really loved my great-grandfather."

Gappy set his jaw in a determined way. "Well, when I'm grown up, I'm going to try and find him, Mom. He must be somewhere."

Dad ruffled his son's hair. "You can do that, Gappy, but I wouldn't hold out much hope. Even the Council couldn't find him."

He stood up. "Are you going to practice some more telekinesis before bed?"

Gappy nodded. "Yeah. I'm gonna try and move the car some more, and then maybe I'll try something a bit heavier, like a book."

After his parents had left the room, Gappy sat down to try some more telekinesis, but he found it difficult to concentrate.

His thoughts kept returning to the great-great-grandfather he had never met. What had happened to him? Was he still alive?

A warm, fuzzy feeling suddenly lodged itself in a piece of Gappy's heart, and his breath caught in his throat as a flash of excitement surged through him. He felt as if a connection had suddenly sprung into being – almost as if a piece of elastic were stretched between his chest and his long-lost great-great-grandfather, pulling at the fibers of his heart.

Gappy gave up trying to concentrate on the car. This was something big. He closed his eyes and let his mind wander. He could almost feel the imaginary piece of elastic vibrating with anticipation. As the warm, fuzzy feeling grew stronger and stronger, his breath caught in his throat again.

With a thrill Gappy opened his eyes. "He's alive," he breathed in wonder. "He's alive!"

He suddenly realized his hands were clenched so tightly that his nails were cutting into the flesh of his palms. He opened them slowly.

"I'll come and find you, Grandpa," he whispered. "One day I'll find you."

Chapter Two

No Adventures This Time!

The next day when Gappy arrived home from school, a big surprise was awaiting him.

"Gappy," his Mother greeted him as he came in the front door, "how'd you like to go visit Llew and Jackie in Wales?"

"No way!" Gappy exclaimed. "For real?"

"Well, your eleventh birthday and spring break are coming up, and your father has to fly over to England to help out the director of the British Council for Underage Dabbling. They've been having some problems with a bunch of unruly vampire kids in Manchester and Evesham. Anyway, we thought you'd like to go too. Uncle Peregrine can meet you at the airport and take you home with him to Wales, and you can spend a whole week with your cousins. It's a sleepy, little village where they live, so you should be able to stay out of trouble."

Livinia Grapple had good reason for saying this. Since Gappy had first found out that he was turning into a vampire like his parents, he had gotten into a few sticky situations and had some dangerous adventures. He had also found himself in trouble with CUD, the Council for Underage Dabbling, for using his powers in public.

Gappy laid out his homework on the kitchen table and hugged himself with glee. What a fantastic birthday present! It would be fun to go overseas and spend a week with his twin cousins. Llewellyn and Jacquelina Abernathy were almost a year older than Gappy. He had met them for the first time last summer when they had flown over with their father, who had business in the States. They had had a great time together at Camp Widdershins, learning all sorts of cool, new vampire skills.

Llewellyn and his father, Peregrine Abernathy, were vampires, but Gappy's Aunt Joelle was a reg, and so was Jackie. Much to her disappointment, Jackie had not inherited the vampire genes, but as Llew's sister she was allowed to attend vampire camp as well. She was looking forward to the day when Llew was able to fly well enough to take her along with him.

Uncle Peregrine called that night to go over the arrangements.

"Gappy," Mom called. "Jackie wants to know if Pru would like to come too. They really hit it off last summer, and she would love to see her again."

"Oh, yes, that would be great, Mom!" Gappy exclaimed. "Can we call Pru's parents right now?"

Dad laughed at Gappy's excited face. "I guess now's as good a time as any."

Gappy crossed his fingers as his father dialed the number and spoke to Pru's mother. There was a pause after Dad told her that Pru had been invited to travel to Wales with Gappy over spring break, and then Gappy heard a faint squeal come through the receiver. His dad gave him a thumbs-up, then spoke some more and invited Pru's parents over to discuss the trip.

He put the phone down at last and turned to Gappy with a grin on his face. "It's all set. Pru's parents have agreed to let her come with us. Her mother just got a big promotion at work, so the air fare is no problem. She'd promised Pru a trip anyway, when the promotion came through, so this works out nicely."

The next day was a Saturday. Pru arrived in the morning, and Gappy took her up to his room while their parents went online to buy airplane tickets and discuss the trip. Pru's mother had met Uncle Peregrine briefly last summer, and she had known Gappy's parents since Gappy and Pru first met in kindergarten. She probably would not be as agreeable to the overseas trip if she knew that Gappy and his parents were vampires and that Gappy and Pru had recently shared in a couple of dangerous adventures.

Last summer the Vampire Council had decided to let Pru in on the vampire secret after she and Gappy had been kidnapped by the Master and Gappy had had to use a vampire skill to help them escape. It could be difficult being a vampire *protector* at times, but Pru took her responsibility very seriously.

Upstairs in Gappy's room the two friends were taking turns examining hairs under Gappy's microscope. Gappy kept glancing sideways at the toy car sitting innocently on his desk. He was bursting to tell Pru that he could move it with his mind, but he managed to keep the news to himself and turn his attention back to the microscope.

"Isn't it funny how a strand of hair has all those scaly things coming off of it?" Pru remarked, screwing up one green eye as she moved one of her bright red hairs around under the viewer. She straightened up after a while. "Why are you so restless, Gappy? Do you need to go to the bathroom?"

Gappy grinned and forced himself to stop fidgeting.

* * * * * * * * * * * * *

The next two weeks dragged by – except for Gappy's birthday, that is – and then it was time to leave for their trip.

That Friday afternoon after school, Mrs. Pottage dropped Pru off at Gappy's house and kissed her goodbye while Gappy's father loaded suitcases into the SUV.

After Pru's mother had driven away, Livinia Grapple hugged her son then held him away from her to look earnestly into his eyes. "No adventures this time, okay, Gappy? I don't want to have to worry about your being kidnapped again or getting into any danger."

Gappy grinned. "I'll try not to, Mom. You said it was a sleepy, little village where Jackie and Llew live, didn't you? There probably won't even be a hint of an adventure. Anyway, if I do see one coming, I'll just wave it right on by."

His mother laughed. "Okay. You do that. Now, I want you to have lots of fun, and say hi to your cousins for me."

The drive to John F. Kennedy Airport took a few hours, and the flight to England took another seven hours. Gappy and Pru were pleased to find video screens in the seat backs in front of them, and after dinner they passed the time watching movies while Mr. Grapple slept.

It was nearly six o'clock in the morning their time when the plane landed at Birmingham Airport, but in England it was nearly eleven o'clock. Uncle Peregrine was waiting for them when they came through customs. Tall and thin with dark hair, he had not changed much since Gappy had met him last summer, except that he had shaved off his long sideburns.

He smiled down at Gappy and Pru, his grey eyes twinkling. "*Bore da*. That means good morning in Welsh," he said. "Lovely to see you both. I'm glad you could come, Pru. It'll be nice for Jackie to have a reg friend along. She wants help knocking some of Llew's corners off. He's joined the gymnastics team at school and thinks he's pretty hot stuff because he can turn somersaults in the air and has a stack of trophies. Jackie's jealous."

Gappy shook his uncle's hand. "Yeah, it's tough being so good at everything," he said with a sideways smirk at Pru. "I often have to make myself lose at games."

Pru kicked him in the shin. "Poor Gappy. It must be such a drag being a vampire and being able to fly and walk through walls, and stuff. Boo hoo!"

Uncle Peregrine laughed and jangled his keys in his pocket.

"That's the spirit. Now, Cuthbert, the rental cars are over there. It'll take you about an hour to get to Evesham where you're going first. We meet back here next Sunday morning, right?"

"That's right," said Cuthbert Grapple, squinting through his glasses to where a sign pointed the way to the car rental. He clapped Gappy on the shoulder. "Bye, Gappy. Remember what your mother said, and stay safe. Bye, Pru. Keep an eye on him, will you?"

"Don't worry," Uncle Peregrine told him. "Abergath is a very small village in the middle of the countryside. Nothing exciting happening there, I'm afraid." He took one of Pru's bags. "Come along then. We've got about a two-and-a-half-hour drive ahead of us, and Llew and Jackie are dying to see you."

"Why didn't they come with you?" Gappy asked as they waved goodbye to his dad and followed his uncle to the parking garage.

"Llew's at a gymnastics meet in the next town, and Jackie's doing some emergency babysitting for a couple in the village," Uncle Peregrine told him. He came to a stop next to a greenish-grey, battered, old station wagon. "Here we are." He unlocked the trunk and heaved their bags into the back.

Gappy and Pru slept most of the way to Abergath. After all, they had been awake all night. They woke up as the station wagon turned onto a rough road and began jolting up and down. Gappy looked out of the window and found himself staring straight down a steep drop into a valley below.

"Whoa, is this safe?" he gasped. "Don't go over the edge, Uncle."

Uncle Peregrine laughed. "You'll have to get used to roads like this in North Wales, my lad. It's very hilly in these parts, and the roads are very narrow."

"Watch out!" Pru squealed as a vehicle approached from

the other direction. "There's only room for one car on this road."

"Och, he'll pull over somewhere and let us pass," said Uncle Peregrine. Sure enough, the other car pulled into a small clearing on the side of the road, and Uncle Peregrine drove by with a wave of thanks to the other driver.

They continued on up the steep road until it leveled out, and soon they could see a little cluster of buildings basking in the sunshine in the valley below.

"That's Abergath," Uncle Peregrine told them. "See? I told you it was quiet."

Sure enough, the village was surrounded by a patchwork of green fields separated by low walls of rough stone pieced together like a jigsaw puzzle. Everywhere the children looked, the fields were dotted with sheep and lambs and yellow gorse bushes. At the far end of the valley the blue waters of the Irish Sea sparkled in the sunlight.

"That's Cardigan Bay," said Uncle Peregrine. "And the small town you can see perched at the end of the valley is Llanafon where Llew has his gymnastics meet. There's an old mansion there where King Charles is said to have hidden in a priest hole, and there are smugglers' tunnels down to the beach."

"Smugglers' tunnels?" said Gappy. "Cool, but what's a priest hole?"

Uncle Peregrine explained. "Well, when Elizabeth the First was Queen of England, Catholics were forbidden to practice their religion, so their priests were forced to travel secretly around the country to bring people the sacraments of the Church. They risked being severely punished if discovered, so people used to build little, secret compartments into their houses where a priest could hide if the Queen's officials came looking for him."

"Wow," Pru breathed, eyes open wide. "I thought this was supposed to be a sleepy, little place, but it sounds exciting."

Uncle Peregrine changed gear as they began to descend into the valley. "Sorry to disappoint you, Pru, but the house isn't open to the public, and the smugglers' tunnels have all fallen in."

They reached the village and drove down the main street past some little stores that sold things like wool, hardware, antiques, and knick knacks. Then came the general store and lastly a cozy little shop called *Maisie's Tea Room*, whose sign declared that the best cream teas in all of Wales could be found there.

Gappy nudged Pru. "We'll have to check that out."

Behind the stores on the main street were a couple of streets with houses built of stone blocks with slate roofs and small windows. Almost as soon as they had entered the village, they were driving out of it again. A little way past the teashop the station wagon turned right and drove past an orchard, a couple of houses, and a field. Then they turned into the driveway of a stone cottage set in the middle of an acre of grass surrounded by flowering bushes.

"Here we are," Uncle Peregrine announced. "Welcome to Perryelle Cottage."

"Hey!" a girl shouted as she burst out of the cottage and galloped down the path to meet them. She enveloped Pru in a big hug. "Hi, Pru, I'm so glad you could come. Uh, you too of course, Gappy," she laughed, hugging him in turn. "Llew!" she yelled over her shoulder. "They're here!"

She threw her blonde ponytail over her other shoulder. "Llew just got back from a gymnastics competition. He won another trophy. I keep telling him it's not fair to the other gymnasts because even though he's not supposed to, I bet he uses his vampire powers to turn all sorts of crazy somersaults."

"I should hope not," remarked Uncle Peregrine, taking

suitcases out of the back of the station wagon.

"Jacquelina Ermintrude, you're just jealous!" a husky voice said as her brother met them at the front door. "Hi, guys. It's lucky we're on school break at the same time, isn't it? We're gonna have some fun. Come upstairs and I'll show you where you'll be sleeping."

Jackie led the way. "You're sharing my room, Pru, and you're bunking in with Llew, Gappy."

"Here, let me take that," said Llewellyn, grabbing hold of Pru's suitcase.

"Ooh, you're such a gentleman, Llew," Jackie teased. "I bet if *I* was lugging a suitcase around, you wouldn't offer to carry it for *me*."

"What's that smell? I'm starving," said Gappy as he heaved his own suitcase up the stairs."

"Mom made sausage rolls," Jackie answered as they reached the landing. "You can just leave your suitcases on your beds and then we'll go downstairs and eat. Here's my room, Pru."

Gappy looked at his watch. "I have to change my watch. It's past nine o'clock in the morning back home. Time for breakfast."

"Well, it's past two o'clock here," Llew said, hefting Pru's suitcase onto one of the beds in Jackie's bedroom. "Time for a late lunch."

Gappy and Pru looked around their rooms quickly and then followed the others downstairs to the kitchen.

Joelle Abernathy straightened up from taking a baking sheet of sausage rolls out of the oven. She smiled at them. "Hello, you two. Gappy, it's nice to finally meet you. Happy belated birthday!

"And you must be Pru. I've heard a lot about you two and your adventures."

"Hi, Aunt Joelle," said Gappy, smiling back at her. His aunt looked like a grown-up version of Jackie, but plump. Her blonde hair was held back from her red face by a couple of pink metal combs, from which strands of hair were doing their best to escape.

"Let me put these on the table, and then I can greet you properly," she said, scooping up the sausage rolls and putting them on a plate. She put the plate down on a big, scrubbed wooden table in the center of the kitchen, then turned and opened her arms. "Give us a hug, then."

As Aunt Joelle wrapped her plump arms around Gappy and Pru, they breathed in the rosy scent of her perfume, and her apron smelled of cinnamon – a funny combination of smells, but nice.

"Can I call you Aunt Joelle too?" asked Pru, hugging her back. "I don't have an auntie of my own."

"Sure you can," Aunt Joelle said, taking off her apron and hanging it over a chair. "Now, let's eat."

As they sat down, Gappy and Pru looked with delight at the spread of food – sausage rolls, homemade bread and butter, a bowl of ripe cherry tomatoes, deviled eggs, and apple pie for dessert.

"Dig in," said Uncle Peregrine, chuckling at their eager faces.

"So, Gappy, tell us about your latest adventure," Llew suggested. "Didn't you run into some crooks in a graveyard, or something?"

"Pru too," Jackie put in. "She was a hero."

"Heroine," Llew corrected her then made a face as Jackie kicked him under the table.

In between bites of warm, flaky sausage roll, Gappy and Pru took turns describing the adventure they had had over winter break.

Llew listened with his mouth wide open. "Wow, Gappy.

You do have a habit of getting into trouble, don't you?" He popped a whole cherry tomato into his mouth.

"I wish *I* could have an adventure like that," Jackie lamented. "Nothing exciting ever happens around here."

"And so it should be," Uncle Peregrine said with a laugh.

"Your poor parents, though, Gappy," said Aunt Joelle, pouring out glasses of grayish-black juice for the vampires at the table and orange juice for herself and the girls.

Pru pointed at Gappy's glass. "Eeuuww, what's that?"

"Adder juice," Llew told her. "You have rattlesnake juice in America; we have adder juice in the U.K. Taste it, Gappy. It's good."

Gappy sniffed the juice then took a tentative sip. "Mmm, yeah. Tastes a bit like rattlesnake, but more spicy. I think I like it."

Jackie wrinkled her nose at Pru. "Yuck, huh?"

Pru nodded with a grin. "Totally gross."

Aunt Joelle chuckled and picked up a large spoon. "Pie, anyone?"

After lunch, Gappy and Pru unpacked their suitcases, and then Jackie and Llew showed them around the house and yard – or, rather, the *garden*, as Llew corrected them. Behind the house was a shallow stream babbling over a bed of pebbles. The water had a greenish tinge to it.

"Why's it that color?" Gappy asked as he leaned over the railing of a rickety bridge.

"It's copper," Jackie told him. "There are copper mines near here."

On the other side of the bridge was a square pond with ducks floating on it and a wire pen with two big, pink-and-grey-mottled pigs. "Say hello to Pinky and Perky," said Llew.

"Are you going to eat them?" Pru asked, looking horrified.

Llew laughed and shook his head. "Don't worry, Pru. Dad

bought them for pets. He thought it would be fun to keep a couple of pigs."

"Why are pigsties always so muddy?" Gappy asked.

"It's the pigs," Jackie explained. "Dad bought these ones 'cause he heard that this type of pig wasn't supposed to dig up the ground. But they still do." She opened a little gate in the stone wall beyond the pig pen. "Let's go look at the lambs."

The rest of the day was spent wandering around the fields behind the house, accompanied by a black-and-white sheep dog.

"This is Dilys," Jackie told them, patting the dog's head. "It means steadfast or true."

"Dill-iss," Pru repeated. "That's pretty. And short. You have such long words in Welsh. All consonants with hardly any vowels."

Llew laughed. "In Welsh, the W's and Y's are vowels though, so that makes it a bit easier. The W is pronounced 'oo', as in 'school', and the Y can have three different sounds – 'ee', 'eye', and 'uh'."

"I guess I've been saying our great-great-grandfather Tristan Glyndwr's name wrong, then," Gappy said. "It's not Glen-*dow*-er?"

"No. In Wales it's pronounced Glin-*doo*-er." Llew said. "But Glendower is the anglicized version, so you're partly right."

"How about Llanfairpwllgwyngyllgogerychwyrndrobwllllantysiliogogogoch?" put in Jackie, showing off her Welsh prowess. "It's a village near here on the island of Anglesey. It has almost the longest name in the world."

"Boy, I won't even try to pronounce *that!*" Pru exclaimed. "What does it mean?"

"The church of St. Mary in the hollow of white hazel trees near the rapid whirlpool by St. Tysilio's of the red cave," Llew rattled off with a grin. "But you can just say Llanfairpwll for short. Try it."

"Sthlan-vire-poossl," Gappy repeated slowly, spraying spit everywhere.

"Eeuuww, Gappy!" Pru protested. "You spat on me, and you're scaring the sheep."

Chapter Three

The Autistic Boy

When Gappy woke up the next morning, the sun was shining in at the window of Llew's bedroom. He looked across at his cousin's bed but it was empty. Then he looked at his watch. "Nine o'clock!" he exclaimed. "Whoa, I slept late!"

He scrambled out of bed and ran to the bathroom then quickly got dressed in jeans and a tee shirt. When he opened the door he almost bumped into Pru, who was walking past.

"Hey, sleepy head," she said. "I overslept too. Must be jet lag. Mmm, breakfast smells good."

They went downstairs to the big kitchen where they found Llew and Jackie eating bowls of cereal.

"Good morning, you two," Aunt Joelle greeted them from the stove. "Fancy some bacon and eggs?"

"Yes, please," Gappy answered. "I'm starving."

Pru laughed. "You always are."

"So, what shall we do today?" asked Gappy, looking with approval at the huge plate of scrambled eggs, bacon, and fried bread Aunt Joelle was placing in front of him.

Llew pushed his cereal bowl aside to make room for his own plate of bacon and eggs. "There's a pond near here. We could take a picnic lunch."

"Good idea," his mother said, pouring out glasses of calves' blood for Llew and Gappy and handing them each some pills. "I'll make you some sandwiches while you make your beds. Did you remember to put your cream on this morning, Gappy?"

Gappy nodded. "It was hard to get used to at first, but now

it's just habit."

Indeed, every morning vampires had to go through the routine of smearing *Reflecto* cream all over their bodies to prevent their reflections from disappearing. They also had to apply special vampire sunscreen to protect their skin from burning in the sunlight. If they should fail to do this and stayed out in the sun too long, they could literally burst into flames.

Pru made a face at Jackie as she watched Gappy and Llew swallow down their vampire vitamins with swigs of calves' blood. "Does it still gross you out seeing your dad and Llew drink that stuff?" she asked her.

Jackie shrugged. "I guess I'm used to it now, but it's still disgusting if I think about it."

As he got up from his chair, Llew wiped his finger around his glass and smeared some blood on Jackie's arm.

"Eeuuww, Llew! I'm gonna get you!" she yelled and charged after her brother as he ducked out of her way. Gappy and Pru laughed and followed them up the stairs.

When they came downstairs again after making their beds, Aunt Joelle handed Llew a backpack. "I've packed you cheese-and-cucumber and tuna sandwiches, juice cartons, chocolate cake, and some apples," she announced. "That should last you for a while. Have fun, and be careful."

"We will," said Llew, slipping his arms through the straps of the backpack. "Thanks, Mom. You're the best."

Gappy hefted another backpack which contained their bathing suits and towels.

The four children wandered out the front gate, turned right, and strolled up the lane in the direction of a small wooded area. After about two hundred yards they came upon a ramshackle old cottage. It looked like it used to be a pretty little place, but no one had done any work on it in a long time. Paint was peeling from the window frames, and a hole in the thatched roof was patched with a piece of green tarpaulin. Roses struggled to grow in the front yard but were losing their battle with the choking weeds.

As the four approached, they could hear someone playing a tune on a violin. They paused for a moment to listen to it.

"Sounds sort of sad and heavy," Pru remarked.

The others nodded. They knew what she meant. The throbbing, long-drawn-out notes made them feel the same way.

Just then the front door of the cottage swung open, and out stepped a scrawny, bleached-blonde woman wearing big curlers under a hair net. She began beating a mat against the front step, but when she noticed the children standing by the gate, she straightened up with a tired sigh.

"And what are you looking at?" she demanded.

"Sorry, Ma'am. We just stopped to listen to the violin music," answered Llew, smiling at her in his charming way. "Who's playing? It sounds awfully good."

The woman managed a sad-looking smile. "That's my son, Cade. Crazy about the violin, he is. His pa won't have none of it though."

"I didn't even know there was a boy living here," said Jackie. "How old is he?"

"He's ten," the woman answered. "He don't get out much, poor lad. He's in a wheelchair, y'see. Hasn't been playing the violin that long, neither. Saw someone playing it on the TV and started hankering after one. They're expensive, though. Luckily I found a secondhand one in that junk shop down the village."

She gave the mat a hearty whack. Dust flew everywhere, making her cough.

"I'm Mrs. Paskin," she said when she had finished coughing. She looked up and down the street in a furtive fashion. "You look like nice children, and Cade hasn't got any friends. Why don't you come in for a bit and visit? If his stepfather comes home, though, you'll have to leave."

The music stopped abruptly, and Mrs. Paskin's mouth turned up in another sad smile. "There, he heard us. Got ears like a hawk, that child does. You'll have to come in now or he'll be disappointed."

She gave the mat another whack and turned to go into the house.

The four children followed her, holding their breaths as they passed through the cloud of dust that hung in the air. Mrs. Paskin led them down a narrow corridor and ushered them into a room at the back of the house. "Here 'e is. Cade, you got visitors."

She bent over a thin boy sitting crookedly in a wheelchair and smoothed his blonde hair away from his forehead. "He doesn't talk much because he's autistic," she whispered to them, "and he can't walk 'cause he was born with spina bifida." She patted Cade's shoulder. "He'll enjoy your company though, I'm sure. I'll let you get acquainted."

She went out and the four children looked at one another, then at the wheelchair-bound boy. He was staring off into a corner of the room and did not seem to have noticed their arrival. His violin lay on a small table next to his wheelchair.

"Let's sit down then," said Llew loudly in an over-cheerful voice. He sat down on a couch in front of the wheelchair and bent to look into Cade's face. "Hi, Cade. I'm Llew. We heard you playing your violin and thought we'd come and say hello."

Cade ignored him and remained staring into the corner, though one finger of his right hand twitched.

Gappy and the girls sat down next to Llew.

"I'm Pru," Pru said, trying to catch Cade's eye.

"I'm Jackie."

"And I'm Gappy."

Cade's right hand twitched again, and his gaze shifted

slightly.

Gappy leaned forward and patted Cade's bony knee. "We'll just sit here for a while and keep you company, okay?"

"And if you want to play your violin, we'd love to hear it," Pru added.

Llew started telling the others about a time when Dilys had lost one of her puppies and they had had to search high and low before they found it trapped upside down in an old boot in the barn.

As the others listened, they kept glancing at Cade. After a while his eyes began to turn in their direction. Eventually he seemed to be looking straight at them but with an empty expression on his face, as if he were looking *through* them. Then in a flash his expression brightened, and with a smile he picked up his violin and played a quick tune.

"Maybe that's his way of showing us he's happy," Pru remarked as she watched the boy's fingers fly over the strings. "He's really good, isn't he?"

Cade finished the tune with a flourish of his bow and returned the violin to the table. Then he smiled sweetly at them and clapped his hands together.

"What's all this noise?" a loud voice suddenly demanded from the doorway as a heavyset man marched into the room. He had swarthy skin, shaggy brown hair, and was wearing a dirty red bandanna around his neck. "What you kids doin' 'ere?"

Gappy and the others jumped up, but not before they noticed a frightened expression swim into Cade's eyes. The boy screwed his eyes shut and began rocking back and forth in his wheelchair.

"Winifred!" the man roared. "What's the meaning of this – letting any old riff-raff into my house?"

His wife scuttled up the corridor like a scared mouse. "I'm sorry, Trevor. Don't yell at them. They're nice children come to visit Cade. You know how lonesome he gets."

"Don't know nuthin' of the sort," the man retorted. "The boy's head is empty. You should have put him in a home years ago."

"Yes, dear," Mrs. Paskin said. "But you know I couldn't do it. He's my own flesh and blood. Anyway, he don't make no trouble for you, does he?"

"What d'ya call that infernal wailing noise, then?" Trevor yelled. "I've a good mind to break that dratted violin over my knee."

"Excuse me, sir," Llew spoke up. "We think Cade's very talented."

"Excuse *me*!" the man roared almost loud enough to raise the roof. "Excuse *me*? My, we are posh, aren't we? You'd do well to mind your own business in someone else's house, boy, you hear? Now get out, the lot of you, and mind your manners."

He caught sight of Cade rocking in his wheelchair. "And stop that sniveling, Cade." And with that, the nasty man turned on his heel and marched out of the room.

Winifred crept in, looking scared. "Thanks for coming," she said in a low voice. "You're nice children. Sorry about my husband. He does love to shout, but he didn't forbid you to come again, did he? I think Cade likes you, and it's good for him to be with other children."

"I don't know, Mrs. Paskin," said Jackie. "We don't want to cause any trouble for you or Cade, or get into trouble ourselves."

"Well, Trevor's out all day tomorrow," Mrs. Paskin told them. "Maybe you could pop in then? Please try. It would be so nice for Cade. Oh, and call me Winnie, if you like – short for Winifred."

Gappy felt sorry for the poor woman. "Maybe we'll come

tomorrow."

The four children left the cottage, passing Trevor on the way. He muttered something under his breath as they went by.

"Charming fellow," Llew commented when they were safely out of earshot.

"Poor Cade," Jackie said. "Fancy having a dad like that."

Everyone was silent for a moment. They felt upset about what they had just witnessed.

"So where's this pond?" Gappy asked after a while, wiping the sweat from his forehead. The sun was beating down on them out of a clear, blue sky. He took a tube of sunscreen from his pocket and smeared some on his nose, which was starting to feel a little prickly. He offered the tube to Llew.

Llew shook his head. "I'm okay for now, thanks." He pointed to the wooded area ahead of them. "The pond's in a little clearing in those woods. It's a bit early in the year for swimming, but the weather's been so warm, the water shouldn't be that chilly. Anyway, it's a nice place for a picnic."

"What's that funny, jagged hill on the other side of the woods?" Pru asked. "I could see it sticking up above the trees when I looked out of our bedroom window."

Jackie stopped to shake a stone out of her sandal. "It's the old Penffordd Slate Mine. They dumped all the stuff they couldn't use on top of the hillside. The mine's been closed for about fifty years, though. I guess the slate wasn't much good."

"Cool," said Gappy. "Are there tunnels we can explore?"

"The entrance is all boarded up," Llew answered, shifting the straps of his backpack on his shoulders, "but there are other mines nearby that are open to the public if you want to go down one."

As they entered the woods, an old, rusty, brown car appeared around a bend in the road ahead. It suddenly screeched to a stop next to them, and the driver rolled down his window.

Chapter Four

A Puzzling Find

"Where you kids headed?" the driver of the brown car demanded in a rough voice. He did not look like a very pleasant character. His scowling face was pitted with acne scars, and he wore a greasy leather cap on his head.

"Just taking a stroll," Llew answered. "Why? Where are you coming from? There's nothing in this direction except the Penffordd Slate Mine. Are you lost?"

"Mind your own beeswax," the man growled. He stuck his arm out of the window and wagged a dirty finger at them. His huge bicep was encircled with a jagged barbed-wire tattoo.

"And stay away from that quarry, you hear? It's dangerous for kids."

Without waiting for an answer, he sneered at them and took off down the road, leaving an oil spot behind him on the pavement.

"Well, that's another unpleasant character," Gappy commented as they continued on into the woods. "Are all the people like that in Wales?"

"Silly," Llew said, but he looked thoughtful. "I wonder where he was coming from though? There's nothing at the end of this road but the mine and a big house that used to belong to the mine owner. The house has been empty for years. Since the mine was all closed up, there was no reason for him to stay."

"Why did that man call it a quarry?" Pru asked. "Is it like a big, open pit?"

"No," said Jackie. "The Welsh often call underground slate

mines quarries too."

"I bet that man was up to something," said Gappy. "Why else would he warn us not to go near the mine?"

"Let's go take a look around and see," Jackie suggested. "We can come back to the pond afterwards for lunch."

Everyone agreed, so they kept on walking along the road through the woods until they reached the other side. Facing them beyond a wide piece of flat, scrubby ground was a huge hill covered in jagged pieces of slate piled all higgledy-piggledy. They looked as if they could slide down the hillside at any moment, though they had obviously been lying in the same place for years because weeds and scrub had grown up around them. A dirt road led around the hill a little way, ending in a small parking lot by some old tumbledown, roofless buildings. Here and there stood rusted railroad carts that the miners had once used to transport slate from the mine. In the side of the hill was an arched entrance, but as Llew had said, it was boarded up tight.

As they came up to it, Gappy examined the heavy planks. They were studded here and there with stout nails. "It doesn't look like anyone has used this entrance in a long, long time," he remarked. "Is there another way in?"

Llew shook his head. "Not that I know of."

"Let's go look at the mine owner's house," Pru suggested, "but quickly, in case Old Greasy Cap comes back."

They walked back the way they had come, then continued along the dirt road which curved around to the back of the hill and ended at a large, stone house. The roof had fallen in at one end, and windows gaped blankly at them as the children approached. Gappy stepped up to the front door and tried the handle, but the door was locked.

"Here's an open window," Jackie called from where she was exploring the side of the house. The others went to join her and found her hoisting herself up onto the windowsill of a window that was missing a pane of glass in its bottom half. "Careful," she warned. "There are some jagged bits of glass at the sides."

"Isn't this trespassing?" Pru asked as Jackie jumped down into the room beyond.

Llew picked up a rock and tried to break off some of the pieces of glass that were sticking out of the window frame. "I told you it's abandoned. The mine owner's dead by now, and no one ever comes here."

"Except maybe the man in the brown car," Pru reminded him.

"I think it's okay if we just take a look," said Gappy. "I mean, look at this place? It's all falling down, and we won't be doing any harm."

"I guess," Pru agreed. "Give me a leg up, then. I'm the shortest."

Once inside the children prowled around looking at the rooms. The house smelt of damp and mildew, and all the rooms on the side where the roof had fallen in were empty. In a back room on the other side, however, they found a sleeping bag on the mildewy carpet next to an open duffel bag stuffed with men's clothes.

"These probably belong to that man," Gappy said. "I wonder what he's doing and how long he's been here?"

"Quite a while, I'd say," Llew called from the next room. "Look at this."

The others joined him and found themselves in a large kitchen. A garbage can filled with pizza boxes and fish-and-chip wrappers stood next to a wooden counter, on which sat a portable stove and a battered tin saucepan of congealed baked beans. An alcove at the side of the kitchen housed an old-fashioned pump, and a tin cup hung from a hook on the wall next to it. Gappy cranked the pump handle, and water splashed out onto the floor.

"Oh, look what you've done!" Jackie exclaimed. "He'll know someone's been here, now."

"Don't worry," Gappy told her. "I saw some old newspapers in another room. We can use them to mop up the water. It's warm in here, so the floor will dry quickly."

"Speaking of warm, I'm hot," Pru complained, fanning her face with her hand. "Let's go outside. There's nothing else to see here. Maybe he's just a homeless squatter."

Gappy found a few sheets of newspaper and mopped up the water. Then he hid the wet pages under the food wrappers in the garbage can.

After they had climbed out of the window again, the children wandered over to look at an old barn behind the house. Here they made another find. Stacked in a corner were several metal bars of varying lengths, some heavy-duty saws and tools, and a couple of welding torches and welding masks.

Llew picked up a big screwdriver and hefted it in his hand. "This stuff looks like it hasn't been here long. It's not covered in dust like everything else is. What's it for?"

"Beats me," said Gappy, kicking one of the sturdy metal bars. "I think these are steel. Looks like someone's been doing some welding."

"But why? What are they making?" Jackie wondered, looking around. "I don't see anything that's been welded."

"It's a mystery," said Pru in a dramatic voice. "We should leave though, before the man comes back."

"Pru's right," Jackie agreed. "I'm sure he wouldn't be happy to find us poking around his stuff. C'mon boys, let's go. I'm ready for a swim."

Llew put the screwdriver down where he had found it. "I guess so."

"We can talk about it while we're eating our lunch," said Gappy. "I'm getting hungry."

As Llew led them back up the road to the woods, they kept an eye out for the man's car, but the road remained empty. As they turned the bend, Llew branched off into the trees, and after a little way they came to a large clearing, in the center of which lay an almost perfectly-round pond.

"This is nice," Pru sighed, plonking herself down on a soft carpet of moss. "Throw me a cheese sandwich, will you, Llew?"

Soon they were all munching sandwiches and discussing their finds at the mine owner's house.

"Maybe he was making a cage for a big animal," Jackie suggested.

"Maybe he belongs to a circus and has to make a cage for a lion," said Gappy.

"Yeah, like there are lots of circuses with lions in this part of Wales," Llew teased. He stretched and gave a huge yawn. "Or maybe we'll never know. How about a swim to cool off, and then we could try a spot of flying?"

Jackie clapped her hands. "Ooh, yes. Gappy, Llew said he would give me a ride when you came. He's been practicing ever so hard since we came back from summer camp last year."

"I've been practicing too," Gappy said. "D'you want a ride, Pru?"

Pru nodded excitedly. "Ooh, yes!"

The children went behind some bushes to change into their bathing suits and then took a dip in the pond. The water felt very cold on their hot bodies, but it was very refreshing. They splashed about for a while and swam a few races. Llew won most of them, as he was the biggest, but the athletic Jackie won the rest.

Afterwards they dried themselves with their towels and got

dressed, and Llew demonstrated some twisty somersaults. He was rather good at it. Although Jackie teased him about cheating, he didn't use his vampire skills when he was competing. "It feels better winning by my own self than cheating by using my powers," he told Gappy.

After a piece of cake each, Jackie and Pru watched enviously as Gappy and Llew tried a few practice flights. Actually they were more like vertical leaps straight up into the air. Both boys managed to shoot themselves up to the level of the tree-tops and hover there for a moment, looking down at the girls below. They both concentrated on imagining whatever method they had found worked best to get themselves into the air and stay there. Gappy imagined himself as a rocket man, with air shooting out of the soles of his shoes, raising him up. Llew, who was fond of surfing, was probably picturing a huge wave sweeping him off his feet and keeping him aloft as he rode along the top of it. He held his arms out wide, as if he were really balancing on a surf board, whereas Gappy kept his arms bent at his sides, palms down, as if pushing against the air.

"How are you doing up there?" Pru yelled, squinting in the sun as she gazed up at the boys.

"Great," Gappy yelled back. "It's a nice view."

"Well, mind no one sees you in the village," Jackie called as the boys began floating down to earth.

Gappy and Llew landed on the mossy ground, their faces flushed from effort and excitement. They both looked pleased with themselves.

"You've improved a lot," Gappy told Llew. "When I saw you last, you could only get up about four inches, remember?"

Llew nodded. "Yeah, thanks."

"Ready for a ride, Pru?" Gappy asked her. "Try standing on my feet with your back to me. Then you'll be able to see where we're going. Let me put my sneakers on first, so you won't hurt my feet."

He bent to tie his sneakers while Pru hopped up and down impatiently.

Jackie also did some hopping up and down of her own while her brother put his sneakers on too. "Are we gonna try that, Llew?"

Her brother straightened up. "Yeah. We'll see if it works."

The girls stepped onto the boys' feet and put their arms behind their backs to hold around the boys' waists.

"Ready?" Gappy said. "I'll count to three. One, two . . ."

"Three!" yelled Llew and went shooting up into the air.

Jackie shrieked in fright as she almost fell off of Llew's feet. She screwed her eyes shut and dug her fingers into her brother's back for dear life.

"Don't worry, I've got you," Llew said into her ear as he squeezed his arms around her. "Relax."

"O-o-o-kay," Jackie managed, just before a pine cone hit her on the head from a nearby branch. She opened her eyes as their ascent slowed and took a look around. The top of the woods looked like a furry, green carpet.

"Don't look down!" Gappy yelled as he hovered nearby with Pru. "You have to get used to it first."

Of course, as soon he said this, both girls immediately looked down.

"Yikes!" Jackie exclaimed and screwed her eyes shut again.

"Whoa!" Pru shrieked. "We're so high up!"

"Well, what did you expect?" Gappy shouted. "I told you not to look down."

Jackie opened her eyes again and looked steadfastly straight ahead.

"Can we move around, Gappy?" Pru asked. "Like circle the clearing?"

"I'll try," said Gappy. He imagined air shooting out of his

shoes at a different angle and began slowly moving forward.

"That's it!" Pru said. "Good, Gappy. It feels like we're really flying now."

"Try it, Llew," Jackie urged her brother.

Llew concentrated on his imagination and began following Gappy.

"This is so cool!" he yelled. "Hey, Gappy, we're really flying!"

"I know!" Gappy yelled back over his shoulder. "Isn't it awesome?"

As the boys finished one lap around the clearing, they began to feel more confident.

"Hey, Pru, you're starting to not weigh anything," Gappy whispered in her ear. "I can hardly feel you on my feet anymore. Let go of me. I think I can hold you by myself."

"Really?" Pru questioned in a doubtful voice. "I'm scared. Can we get closer to the ground first? Then if you drop me, I won't have so far to fall."

Gappy agreed and began sinking in the air.

"What are you doing?" Llew called.

"I think something's happening," Gappy called back. "Pru doesn't weigh anything anymore. She's going to try letting go."

"Wow, you're right!" Llew exclaimed. "Jackie doesn't feel as heavy anymore either. I'll follow you."

He sank downwards until he was hovering a few feet above the mossy ground near Gappy.

Pru gingerly let go with one arm. A few seconds later, not noticing any difference in Gappy's ability to support her, she let go with the other arm as well.

"It works!" she and Gappy yelled together.

"Your turn," Llew said in Jackie's ear.

His sister cautiously let go with one arm and then the other.

"We can do it too!" she yelled excitedly.

"Now, what happens if *I* let go with one arm?" Gappy wondered aloud. Before Pru could protest, he held out one arm to the side like a one-winged airplane. "Look. I'm only holding you with one arm now."

"Er, yeah," Pru said. "It's weird but it feels okay."

After a few seconds, when she still felt safe, she stretched out both of her arms. "Let's go flying!"

Holding Pru around her waist with one arm, Gappy flew a practice lap around the pond, then began rising higher in the air as he flew another lap. After a while he found that he could lean forward even more until he was lying almost flat in the air with Pru beneath him.

Pru kept her arms stretched out on either side and yelped with delight as they zoomed around the clearing. "This is great!" she screamed, bright red hair streaming out behind her. "This is what I call real flying. Wooooooooooh!"

Gappy dodged his head sideways to avoid Pru's hair. "Yeah, it's times like this when it's so cool being a vampire," he yelled.

"And I'm so lucky to have a vampire for a best friend," Pru yelled back. "The girls at school would kill to be able to do this."

Hearing Llew and Jackie whooping excitedly behind them, Gappy slowed down a little so they could catch up. Jackie looked as if she were swimming a weird kind of breaststroke in the air, while Llew held out one of his arms to the side like Gappy was doing, his other arm around his sister's waist.

As their delighted passengers urged them on, the boys began zigzagging in front of each other as they flew. They had the time of their lives, whooping and hollering to each other as they zoomed around the clearing, the wind whistling in their ears.

After a while everyone started to feel dizzy from flying clockwise, so Gappy and Llew changed direction and began flying the other way. However, changing direction proved to be more difficult and took quite a bit of extra work.

"It's like when you're at a skating rink, and everyone's skating in one direction, and then they suddenly tell you to turn and skate in the other direction," Llew panted. "I always find that hard to do."

"I'm ready to stop, anyway," Gappy called, beginning to sink lower. "This is tiring."

As soon as he landed on the mossy carpet, Pru leaped off of his feet and gave him a big hug. "That was great, Gappy!" she exclaimed, her eyes shining.

Llew and Jackie landed just then, and Pru ran over to them. She flung her arms around Jackie, and they jumped up and down together.

"We're the luckiest girls in the world!" Pru shrieked.

"You know it!" Jackie yelled back.

Llew and Gappy grinned at each other. "Pretty cool, huh, *pardner?*" said Llew, trying to sound American.

"Pretty cool."

Chapter Five

The Hidden Map

Next morning everyone woke to the sound of rain pattering against the window panes.

"I suppose this means we can't go down to the beach, then," Llew complained, looking out the window.

Gappy laughed at his expression. "Cheer up, Llew. It's only our second day here. There's lots of time left."

Someone knocked on the door just then, and Jackie walked into the boys' bedroom.

"Jackie, how many times have I told you to wait for me to say 'come in'?" Llew grumped at her. "Oh . . . hello, Pru."

"Do you want to go down to the village and explore that old junk shop?" said Pru, who had followed Jackie into the room. She bounced on Gappy's bed. "It looked like there were some interesting things in there when we drove past the other day. We brought umbrellas with us. It rains a lot in the U.K. doesn't it?"

Llew looked a bit more cheerful. "Yeah. We've got umbrellas as well. We could have some scones and jam at Maisie's Tea Room too."

"Let's go visit Cade first," Jackie suggested. "I saw his dad walking down the road just now, and his mom did say she wanted us to visit."

After breakfast the four children waved goodbye to Aunt Joelle and set off up the street to Cade's house, walking single file beneath their umbrellas.

Winifred Paskin met them at the door with one of her tired

smiles. "Hello, kids," she greeted them, placing a hand over her other arm to cover up a large bruise. "Thanks for coming. Cade will be pleased."

She led the way to the room at the back of the house and opened the door. As they filed in, they found Cade sitting in his wheelchair. He had a large, purple bruise on his cheekbone.

"How did you both get those bruises?" Pru asked.

Winnie hesitated for a moment, then touched her red, scrubbed fingers to Cade's cheek. "Oh, Trevor got a little bad tempered last night, didn't he, love? He can be a bit free with his fists sometimes."

The four children looked shocked. "That's awful!" Gappy exclaimed. "You should have him arrested."

"Yeah, I know," Winnie said sadly. "I'll think about it."

Cade was gazing off to his favorite spot in the corner of the room. For an awkward moment everyone just stood there, feeling embarrassed.

"Well, I've got to go do some cooking," Winnie said at last. "Have a nice visit."

She disappeared down the corridor, and the four children sat on the couch in front of Cade's wheelchair. It was difficult to feel cheerful after hearing about Trevor's behavior and looking at Cade with his bruised cheek. They made an effort, however, and chatted in cheerful voices about this and that. After a while Cade began darting glances at them from under his eyelashes. He even smiled a few times. Then he suddenly picked up his violin and played a little tune.

"Aw, he's showing us he's happy we're here," said Pru. She smiled at Cade. "We're your friends, Cade. Gappy and I are just here on vacation, but when we've gone home, Jackie and Llew will still visit you, I'm sure."

Jackie and Llew nodded their heads. "Of course we will," said Jackie.

"Do you think it's a map?" asked Gappy.

"Yes, you're our friend now, Cade, and friends have to stick together," Llew added, leaning over to pat Cade's shoulder. Cade smiled and awkwardly laid his violin down on the side table.

"Hey, what's this?" Llew asked, spying something white on the seat of Cade's wheelchair as the boy shifted sideways. "You're sitting on something, fella."

He eased out a folded, crumpled sheet of paper from beneath Cade's skinny thigh.

"What is it?" Jackie asked.

"I dunno," said Llew. "Let's take a look."

He unfolded the paper and smoothed it flat on his lap. The others craned their necks to see what it was.

A diagram had been drawn on the paper in bold, black pen. It looked like the outline of a tree trunk with branches sticking out of it on both sides. Some of the branches joined up at different points, making a kind of maze. Here and there circles had been drawn next to the lines, some smaller than others. Some of the circles were marked with an X.

"Do you think it's a map?" asked Gappy.

"Or a drawing of a weird apple tree," said Pru. "Maybe Cade drew it."

She held up the piece of paper so Cade could see it. "Did you draw this, Cade?"

Either Cade was having a good day, or he was getting used to his new friends, because he seemed to be more alert and aware of his surroundings that morning. He looked at the paper and then at Pru, shook his head slightly, and grunted something in a faint whisper.

"I think he said no," said Pru. "Is that right, Cade?"

Cade nodded slightly and flapped his hands up and down.

"Okay, then," said Llew. "If Cade didn't draw it, maybe it is a map."

Cade flapped his hands again.

"Look, he agrees with you," said Gappy. "It's a pity you don't talk, Cade. You could tell us what it is. You probably understand what's going on around you though, don't you?"

Cade looked at Gappy and twitched a finger, then closed his eyes.

"So, if it *is* a map," said Pru, "what would it be a map of?"

"The Penffordd Slate Mine?" Jackie suggested. "Look at these boxes drawn underneath the tree shape. They're arranged like those buildings near the mine entrance. And this box over here would be the mine owner's house."

"I think you're right, sis," Llew agreed. "Now, why would there be a map of the mine hidden under Cade's butt? And why would Trevor or Winnie draw a map of the mine in the first place?"

"If anyone's up to something bad, I bet it's Trevor," Gappy remarked. "Winnie seems too nice to be involved in anything shady."

Pru nodded. "I agree. Maybe Trevor and that man who's staying at the mine owner's house are doing something down in the mine."

"But why would Trevor leave the map underneath Cade?" Llew asked again. "Seems a silly place to hide something important like that."

"Maybe Trevor was looking at it and heard Winnie coming, so he quickly shoved it under Cade to hide it and then forgot about it," said Gappy.

"Let's copy the map," Jackie squealed suddenly, looking excited. "Then we can put the original back where we found it."

"Good idea," said Gappy. "Then we can find a way to get into the mine."

"You promised your mom you wouldn't get into any danger, Gappy," Pru reminded him. "Remember? You said if an adventure appeared, you'd wave it on by."

Gappy brushed her off with a flap of his hand. "I know. We'll just have to be careful, that's all."

"It's all right, Gappy," Llew put in. "This isn't just *your* adventure. It belongs to all of us. We'll just leave you at home if things look like they're getting dangerous."

"Oh no you won't," Gappy protested. "You can't leave me out of it."

Jackie laughed. "It's okay, Gappy. He's just teasing. We'd better copy the map before Trevor comes back. There's some paper and pencils over there on that desk."

She put the map down on a coffee table and laid a blank sheet of paper on top of it. The black-inked lines were dark enough that it was quite easy to trace them. Llew angled a nearby lamp to throw more light onto the table to help Jackie see better.

While she worked on her tracing, the children heard the sound of a vacuum cleaner being turned on nearby.

"Hurry, Jackie," Pru urged.

"I'm going as fast as I can," said Jackie, quickly tracing lines and circles.

The vacuuming came closer and closer. At any moment Winnie might open the door and see what they were doing. Jackie's pencil flew over the paper as the others watched anxiously.

Just as the vacuum reached the door, Jackie finished her task. She folded the copy she had made and stuck it in the pocket of her jeans. Llew quickly folded the original map and managed to slide it back beneath Cade's thigh in the same position he had found it.

"Sorry, buddy," he murmured, but Cade seemed to have disappeared into his own world again.

The door opened and Winnie pushed an old vacuum

cleaner into the room. She wiped a stray hair back from her forehead and smiled at them. "Had a nice visit?" she asked.

"Yes, thank you," said Pru. "Cade played his violin for us."

"What did I tell you?" Winnie exclaimed, looking delighted. "He likes you. Please come again."

"We will," said Jackie, getting up. "Come on, guys."

The children said goodbye to Winnie and Cade and set off down the street to the village. It had stopped raining, and the sun was trying to come out. The road's surface had begun steaming. As they walked along, the four children discussed the map and what Trevor and the other man could be up to.

"Of course, it could be something quite ordinary," Gappy said, kicking a pebble ahead of him. "Maybe they got permission to reopen the mine."

Jackie shook her head. "I wouldn't think so. Everyone knows everyone else's business around here. We'd have heard of it. Anyway, the mine closed because the slate wasn't good enough."

"Jackie's right," Llew agreed. "I think Trevor and that man are crooks. They're up to something, and I want to find out what it is. Hey! Isn't that Old Greasy Cap's car outside Maisie's Tea Room?"

"Shoot," Pru complained. "Let's go to the junk shop first then."

"No, I think we should go in," said Gappy. "We can keep an eye on him."

The girls looked doubtful, but Llew was all for it. "Good idea," he said, steering Jackie toward the door. "No man's going to stop me from getting my tea."

"Oh, Llew," said Jackie, laughing, but she went past him into the tea room as he held the door open for her.

Trevor and the man in the greasy leather cap were sitting together at a table in the back of the tea room. They both scowled at the children. "What you lot doin' 'ere?" Trevor growled.

"It's a free country, sir. We came to have our tea, same as you," answered Llew in an over-polite voice. "We won't bother you."

Trevor grunted and waved to a table by the window. "Sit over there, then. We don't want noisy kids interrupting our conversation."

"Oh, I don't know. I'm sort of partial to this table in the middle of the room," Llew answered airily. He looked around at the others. "Don't I always like to be in the middle of things, guys? Middle this, middle that?"

The others nodded, trying not to giggle, though the men's glowering expressions made them nervous.

"I like middle things too," Gappy announced, pulling out a chair. "It's an American thing."

Trevor's companion snorted and muttered something behind his hand to Trevor. The children watched warily as Trevor got up and waved a finger at them. They waited for him to storm over to their table, but it seemed he was merely changing chairs, because he sat down heavily on a different one with his back to them.

"Oh, the view is *so* much better now," Llew proclaimed in a loud voice.

"What's that, Master Abernathy?" said a large, round woman, bustling through a curtained opening at the back of the tea room. "Not being rude are you?"

"Who me?" Llew demanded, pointing to his own chest. "Never."

The woman's brown eyes twinkled. "You're a cheeky young devil, you are. Now, what will you kids be wanting? I see you've got some friends visiting you."

"Cream teas for four, please, Maisie," Jackie ordered after

introducing Gappy and Pru.

"Right you are," Maisie beamed. "Back in a jiff." And she bustled back through the curtain.

"She's nice," Pru remarked.

"Yes, very," Jackie agreed. "She knows everyone in the village, too. If you need to know what the latest gossip is, ask Maisie."

"Let's ask her if she's heard anything about the mine being bought or sold," suggested Gappy in a soft voice so that the men at the other table would not hear.

Llew nodded. "Good idea, but let's wait until Trevor and Greasy Cap have left."

"Look at them with their heads together," said Jackie. "I wish we could hear what they're saying, but they're talking too softly."

"Yeah, even with my vampire hearing it's hard to make out any words with that music playing on the radio," said Gappy. "They're probably up to mischief."

"Mischief? Who's up to mischief?" asked Maisie in a cheery voice, placing plates of scones, butter, and pots of thick yellow cream and strawberry jam on their table.

"You know us kids, Maisie," Llew answered, smiling up at her kindly face. "Always up to some mischief or other."

The plump woman set a steaming pot of tea before each of them. "As long as it's not in *my* shop," she chuckled. "Enjoy. I'll be in the back if you need me."

Everyone enjoyed their scones immensely, accompanied by mugs of hot tea. "Welsh tea seems so much stronger than the tea we have at home," Pru commented. "I need lots of milk and sugar in mine."

Just then the door to the teashop opened, and a tall man entered. He was bundled up in a dark blue raincoat and scarf and wore a wide-brimmed, floppy black hat crammed down low on his forehead so that it threw his face into shadow. Without hesitation, he strode right past the children and headed straight for Trevor's table. As Trevor and his pal half stood up from their chairs to greet him, the man sat down in Trevor's old chair. Then all three put their heads together and began discussing something in low voices.

The children looked at one another and shrugged.

"Curiouser and curiouser," whispered Pru.

"That is the question," Llew added.

Jackie laughed. "Those quotations don't go together, Llew. One's from *Alice in Wonderland* and the other's from Shakespeare's *Hamlet*."

Llew shrugged. "Whatever, Miss Smarty Pants."

As they ate their scones and sipped their tea, the children kept an eye on the three men. After a few minutes the tall one stood up and put his hand in the inside pocket of his coat. He drew out two envelopes and passed them to Trevor and his companion. Then he muttered something, crammed his hat down lower on his forehead, and quickly strode past the children's table and out of the teashop.

As the door closed, Trevor caught the children looking his way and scowled at them. "Wot you looking at?" he demanded. "Mind your own business, see?"

He turned to his friend. "C'mon, Rhys. Let's go."

Rhys did not say anything, but cast a dirty look at the children. The unpleasant man seemed to own quite a collection of scowls.

Chapter Six

Crooked Stones

As the door closed behind the two men, Gappy and the others let out big sighs. "I feel like I can relax now," said Jackie, stretching.

Gappy nodded. "I know what you mean."

Llew went to the counter and rang a little bell to summon Maisie. She soon appeared, wiping her hands on her apron.

"The cream teas were scrumptious as usual, Maisie," Llew told her. "How much do we owe you?"

Maisie rang up the bill, and everyone chipped in to pay for the teas.

"Heard any gossip lately?" Jackie asked, putting on her jacket. "Any new people in town?"

The round woman tilted her head to one side. "Not much gossip, no. There've been a few new faces around here recently, but they seem to keep to themselves and not bother anyone."

"Do you think anyone's ever going to buy the mine or the mine owner's house?" Llew asked.

Maisie shook her head. "No, I wouldn't think so. The mine's no good, and I don't think anyone would be interested in that old house stuck out there all by itself. Must be in pretty bad shape by now."

The four children waived goodbye to Maisie and crossed the street to the junk shop. They spent a pleasant half-hour browsing around the store, looking at a huge collection of musty old books, ornaments, antique furniture, jewelry, and as-sorted knick knacks and souvenirs. Pru bought a magnet for her fridge back home to remind her of her trip. It was a carved, red dragon, poised above the letters C-Y-M-R-U, the Welsh word for 'Wales'.

After leaving the junk shop, they walked back home enjoying the sunshine. It was beginning to win its battle with the rain clouds.

"What do you want to do this afternoon?" Gappy asked. "Shall we go back to the slate mine and try to find a way in? We'd take the map with us, of course."

Jackie patted the map in her jeans pocket. "Yeah, we should."

"We'll have to keep an eye out for Trevor and Rhys, though," said Llew.

Uncle Peregrine, however, had other plans for them that afternoon. Over lunch he announced that he was taking them for a drive to visit an ancient ring of stones.

"It's called Creigiau Gwyrgam. That means Crooked Stones," Uncle Peregrine explained to Gappy and Pru. "You've heard of Stonehenge in England, haven't you? Well, there are similar stone circles dotted all over Wales. They date back to civilizations that lived here thousands of years ago. We don't really know what they were used for, but some think the stone circles were shaped in a certain way to act kind of like gigantic sundials to track the seasons and let people know when to plant their crops or move south for the winter. They may have been used for religious ceremonies too."

The children nudged one another under the table. It seemed the Penffordd Slate Mine would have to wait for another day.

The drive to Creigiau Gwyrgam took about an hour. Uncle Peregrine drove the car as close as he could get to the stone circle, and then they had to travel the rest of the way on foot. The sun was shining brightly now, and Gappy began to feel hot as he trudged along a narrow sheep's track up a steep, grassy hill, on top of which stood Creigiau Gwyrgam. As he looked at the view around him, all he could see were similar hills surrounding the one he was on and fields of grazing sheep. Birds sang merrily overhead, enjoying their newly-washed world that sparkled in the sunshine from a million rain droplets trembling on a million blades of grass.

Everyone was out of breath by the time they reached the top of the hill. "Here we are," Uncle Peregrine announced. "As you can see, Creigiau Gwyrgam is made up of a circle of twenty tall stones, surrounded by a bank of small rocks. It's really remarkably intact for having stood here for thousands of years exposed to the elements and the shifting of the earth."

Gappy scrambled up the bank of rocks and down the other side, entering the circle between two big boulders. All the standing stones were leaning backwards a little, as if retreating from the center, and were much taller than him.

As he wandered around the circle on the sheep-cropped grass, he gradually began to sense something. He paused to try and figure out just what this new sensation was and suddenly felt a kind of pull in the gut of his stomach, as if something were gently urging – no, tugging him, like a big magnet – toward the center of the circle.

Gappy looked around for the others, but no one else had yet climbed over the bank to join him. He could hear them calling to one another as they explored the outside of the circle. As he drew closer to the center, Llew's words came back to him, "*Middle this, middle that,*" and he chuckled at the memory.

But then he stopped smiling.

The sound of the others' voices had grown suddenly muffled, as if Gappy's head were wrapped in a thick fog or cotton wool. The air suddenly felt thick and heavy too, deadening out even the sounds of the songbirds and the humming of insects.

But, what was that?

Beneath the silence, he could hear – no, feel – a low humming. It was almost more of a vibration than a sound.

Gappy looked around and realized that he was standing in just about the very center of the stone circle. The humming/vibration seemed to be coming at him from all directions. Could the stones be doing the humming? No, really?

Sit down, the feeling urged him, so Gappy sank down and sat cross-legged on the damp, green turf.

He closed his eyes and laid his hands on his knees, palms facing upward, like he had seen people do on TV when they were meditating. He forced himself to breathe in and out slowly and to concentrate. He was not really sure what he was supposed to be concentrating on, but it felt like the right thing to do.

After meditating for about a minute, the image of his great-great-grandfather floated into his mind's eye. Well, no, Gappy couldn't actually see him, and he did not know what he looked like – it seemed more like he was making a connection with the *spirit* of Tristan Glyndwr.

As the thick, heavy air pressed down on him, Gappy's chin sank toward his chest and a great peace came over him. He felt as if he could almost hear some whispered words deep in his brain.

Gappy, my great-great-grandson. You and I are alike. You have gifts. Use them wisely, Gappy. When it's time. I wish . . . I look . . . forward to . . .

"Hey, what are you doing?" a voice yelled, breaking into Gappy's thoughts.

The heavy air instantly lifted, along with the whispery words in Gappy's head. He looked up, blinking in the sunshine.

His cousins and Pru were standing around him, looking at him.

"What were you doing?" Pru asked again. "You looked as if you were in a trance or something."

Gappy shook himself more awake and scrambled to his feet. Shoot! Now his butt was all wet from sitting on the damp ground.

"I dunno," he said. "Something weird just happened. I was walking around the circle, when the air suddenly got all sort of heavy and quiet. And then this weird humming noise or vibration started up – almost like the stones were singing to me. Then something told me to sit down. So I did. And when I closed my eyes, I started hearing words in my head, like my great-great-grandpa Tristan was talking to me."

Pru and Jackie were staring at him with their mouths open wide, but Llew gave a snort.

"Gappy, he's been gone for a hundred years. You must have imagined it. And singing stones . . . ? That's crazy."

"Maybe not," said Uncle Peregrine, who had wandered over to join the group. "Creigiau Gwyrgam was always a special place for Tristan. He used to come here a lot to think and meditate when he was working on improving the New Order of Vampires."

"Whoa, Uncle Perry!" exclaimed Gappy. "So you think he really was talking to me?"

Uncle Peregrine gave a wistful smile. "I'd like to think so, Gappy, but I don't know. As Llew said, he's been gone for a hundred years, and he wasn't even in this country when he disappeared. Maybe you were just picking up some traces of energy he left behind because he used to come here so often. It's odd that you should hear the stones singing to you though. Tristan used to claim he could hear them singing too, but people always said it was his imagination."

Pru patted Gappy on the back. "Cheer up, Gappy. I believe you."

"When I'm grown up, I'm going to look for my great-great-grandpa Tristan," Gappy declared as he followed the others to a sunny spot on the edge of the circle to have a snack. "I want to try and find out what happened to him."

"I doubt you'll be successful, but you can count me in," Llew told him. "It would be fun to do some investigating."

After some cookies and juice the four children wandered around the circle, examining the stones. They strained their ears to try and hear a humming noise, but no one heard anything, not even Gappy. As Gappy thought more about his *quiet time*, as he put it, he began to feel as if he might have just dozed off for a moment and dreamed the whole thing.

Funny we both heard the stones humming, though, he thought. Certainly nothing seemed odd about Creigiau Gwyrgam now. It was just a circle of leaning stones, basking in the sun on the top of a lonely hill.

Chapter Seven

A Moonlit Ride

Late that night, when everyone else was asleep, Gappy was suddenly awakened by the sound of a car driving past the cottage. He lay on his back for a moment, feeling hot and thirsty, as the air was warm and stuffy in Llew's bedroom. Gappy decided he would get a drink of water from the sink in the corner and open the window to let in some air.

He quietly filled a glass of water and drank some, then placed it on the bedside table in order to open the window. As he parted the curtains, he suddenly saw movement out of the corner of his eye and looked up the street towards Cade's house. He could see it quite clearly in the darkness with his sharp vampire eyesight.

A car was parked in front of the house, and as Gappy watched, two men left the building and walked rapidly over to it, looking around them as they did so. They got into the car and slowly eased the doors shut, as if trying not to make a sound. Then the car started up and drove slowly up the street without any lights. The driver waited until entering the woods before turning them on.

Gappy gulped down the rest of his water then shook Llew in the next bed. "Llew, wake up. I just saw something strange."

His cousin rolled over and looked blearily at Gappy in the darkness. "Wha–?" Then he peered at the bedside clock. "It's midnight! Are you crazy?"

"No," Gappy persisted, shaking Llew again as he tried to roll back onto his side. "Cade's dad is up to something. I just saw someone come and get him in their car. It was probably Rhys – Old Greasy Cap – because the engine sounded the same. You know – that put-putting noise it was making when it passed us yesterday? The car was driving without its lights on too, until it got to the woods. Then they came on. Trevor and Rhys must be going to the mine or the mine owner's house."

Llew sat up in a hurry. "Gosh! Good job, Gappy. Go wake the girls."

Gappy went to Jackie's room and shook the sleeping girls' shoulders. "Wake up and come into Llew's room," he told them softly. "Something's going on."

Pru and Jackie woke up much faster than Llew had done. They got out of bed and followed Gappy into Llew's bedroom, looking excited. They found Llew staring out the window.

"So, what's up?" Jackie asked, making herself comfortable on her brother's bed. "Why'd you wake us up in the middle of the night?"

Gappy told them what he had seen. "So what do you think we should do?" he finished.

"Follow them, of course," stated Pru in a determined whisper. "We have to see what they're up to."

"I think so too," Llew agreed. "It'll be an adventure. Er, speaking of adventures, you'd better stay behind, Gappy. No adventures for you."

Gappy dismissed the idea with a brush of his hand. "Forget *that*. I have to come along to protect you, don't I? My mom would never forgive me if I let you get into danger by yourselves."

"So who's going to protect *you*?" Llew teased.

Jackie bounced up and down on her brother's bed, brimming with impatience. "Stop it, you two. Seriously though, we'd better get dressed if we're going to follow them. They've got a car, and we'll have to walk."

"Couldn't we fly?" said Pru.

Gappy and Llew looked at each other. "I don't really feel confident enough to fly at night," Gappy said. "Do you, Llew?"

Llew shook his head. "Unh, unh. We've only just learned how to fly with passengers too, and . . . I don't know . . . it seems different at night. We won't have to walk though. Jackie and I have bicycles."

He pulled yesterday's tee shirt on over his head. "You and I will ride them, Gappy, 'cause we're stronger. The girls can ride on the back on the luggage rack thingies."

The girls rushed next door to get dressed and soon returned to the boys' room. Jackie had a couple of flashlights with her. The four children crept downstairs to the kitchen where Llew eased back the bolt on the outside door and turned the key.

"This door is much quieter to open," he muttered over his shoulder. "The front door's way too noisy."

Once outside, with the door shut softly behind them, they walked over to the garden shed, and Jackie eased open the heavy door. It squeaked a little but not loud enough for anyone in the house to hear.

The boys wheeled the bicycles to the road, then Gappy mounted Jackie's bike and held it still for Pru to settle herself on the back. Llew did the same for Jackie.

"Here we go," Llew breathed. "I think my eyesight's nearly as good as yours, Gappy. We should be able to see well enough in the light from the moon and stars without having to put our bike lamps on."

With the girls perched uncomfortably on the metal racks behind them, Gappy and Llew began pedaling up the street. It was hard work with the girls' extra weight on the back, but it became easier once they got going, and they soon got into the rhythm of it.

The boys pedaled silently past Cade's house. All the windows were dark, and Gappy wondered if Cade and his mother were asleep, or if they knew that Rhys had come to get Trevor and driven away with him, secretly, in the middle of the night.

Once they entered the woods, it became more difficult to see where they were going, especially in the parts where the trees curved over the road, shutting out the moonlight. For the girls, of course, it was pitch dark. They just had to hold on and leave the rest up to Gappy and Llew.

The boys were panting quite hard by the time they reached the other side of the woods. Luckily from that point on the road sloped gently downhill toward the Penffordd Slate Mine, so they had a chance to catch their breaths as they coasted for a while. They took care to keep to the side of the road so they would be able to quickly duck into cover if they heard the men's car approaching. At last they reached the mine and stopped behind some bushes at the side of the road to discuss what to do next.

Llew pointed to a large, tumbledown building nearby. "There's the car. You can just see the back of it sticking out of that big shed. The road turns to dirt soon and gets all potholey. Let's leave the bikes behind these bushes and go take a look around."

Gappy nodded in the darkness. "Be careful, though. You girls keep close to Llew and me. We don't want to use the flashlights unless we have to."

"All right," Pru breathed excitedly. "Shall we go and look at the entrance to the mine and see if it's open now?"

The others agreed and they continued along the road, the girls holding onto the backs of the boys' tee shirts. The road curved to the left and then became the wide dirt road. They stayed in the shadows as much as possible and kept their eyes and ears open for any sign of Trevor and Greasy Cap Rhys.

They soon reached the cluster of buildings and continued on to the mine entrance in the side of the hill. Alas, it looked just as tightly boarded up as it had the day before.

"Darn it," Jackie muttered, giving the rough boards a few experimental tugs. "It doesn't look like they got in this way."

Gappy examined the sturdy, nail-studded planks. "I could probably rip out a couple of these boards if I tried hard enough. Or I could try and particalize through them. But with all these nails I'd probably tear myself to bits. I can't walk through metal yet. What do you think, Llew?"

Llew shook his head. "I wouldn't risk it. It's obvious no one's been using this entrance."

"We walked around the hill to the right the other day," Pru said, "and didn't see any obvious way in, so maybe we should go left this time."

"But why would the men park in the shed if the entrance is even farther past this one?" Gappy pointed out. "If they had to go farther left around the hill, why not park in the parking lot so they'd be closer?"

"You're right," Llew agreed. "If there is another entrance, it's probably in the side of the hill to the right somewhere, closer to the shed. Let's walk slowly round that way, next to the hill this time. The men might have uncovered a hidden entrance that we didn't notice before. Be careful, girls. There's a lot of slate lying around. We don't want any twisted ankles."

Clutching onto the boys' tee shirts again, Jackie and Pru tried to follow in the boys' footsteps, but they found it very hard going in the darkness. Even Gappy and Llew found it difficult because there was so much rubble and debris underfoot.

"It's no use," Jackie hissed after they had gone about twenty feet. "If I stub my toe one more time, I'm gonna scream."

"Me too," Pru agreed. "Can't we use the flashlights, Llew?"

"Too dangerous," Llew answered as they stopped to reconsider. "Jackie's right, though. It's too difficult scouting around the edge of the hill where there's no path and we have to keep dodging all this slate. One of us is going to twist an ankle. It's too noisy anyway, walking on all these crunchy stones,"

As the four children huddled in the darkness wondering what to do next, a faint light suddenly shone out from inside the shed, and they heard a low murmur of voices.

There was nowhere to hide, and they were too scared to move for fear of the men hearing their crunching footsteps.

"Get down and stay still, everyone," Llew breathed softly. "We're far enough away that they shouldn't be able to see us if we don't move. Squint your eyes shut, though, so they don't reflect the light. We don't want the men to see four pairs of eyes staring at them."

Everyone crouched down and screwed their eyes to slits, hardly daring to breathe as they squinted toward the shed. They heard the sounds of more talking, then two car doors slammed shut, and an engine rumbled into life. Gappy and Llew nudged each other as they heard the familiar put-putting sound.

The car's lights came on, and it slowly backed out of the shed. When it was all the way out, it swung to the right and took off up the road. As the rear lights disappeared into the woods, the children breathed sighs of relief.

"So, what now?" Pru asked. "Do you still want to keep looking for an entrance? We can use the flashlights now, can't we?"

"I don't actually think there's an entrance in the hill this way either," Gappy said. "We'd have heard the men crunching about on the stones and seen their flashlights."

"Why don't we go and explore the shed?" Jackie suggested. "After all, the first time we saw a light was when the men were in there. Maybe there's another entrance to the mine inside the shed."

"Good idea, Jackie," Gappy said, patting her arm. "I think the coast is clear now. We can probably use the flashlights to get back to the path."

Jackie and Pru thankfully turned on their flashlights, although they cupped the ends with their hands so the bulbs would not glow too brightly. They picked their way across the rough, stony ground to the dirt road. When they reached it, and the going got a bit easier, Gappy told the girls to turn their flashlights off again, just in case someone else was about. The children linked arms and walked up the road to the big shed. It had no doors, and they were able to walk right inside.

Llew stopped the others at the entrance. "Shouldn't one of us keep watch in case Trevor or Rhys comes back?"

No one wanted to be the guard, so they did rock-paper-scissors, and Jackie lost. With a reluctant sigh she stayed by the door while the others began searching the shed.

The front half of the building was quite empty, with no sign of any possible entrance to a tunnel. The back half was piled with hefty, greasy-looking wire ropes and rusted pieces of mining equipment. Gappy, Llew, and Pru poked about as best they could, getting thoroughly filthy in the process. Gappy's tee shirt soon sported a huge, black, tarry grease stain down one side, and Llew must have rubbed his nose with a grubby hand because he looked as if he were wearing a lopsided, black moustache.

"Find anything yet?" Jackie hissed after a while from her post by the entrance. She had to stand with her back to them to watch for anyone coming but kept glancing over her shoulder to see what progress the others were making.

"Not yet," Pru called back. "There's so much junk back here and it's so dirty!"

"Let me take a turn then," Jackie volunteered. "I don't mind a little dirt."

Pru agreed and they swapped places.

The first thing Jackie did was push against a rusted cart that stood next to the left-hand wall near the back of the shed. With a protesting screech, it moved slowly backwards on its stiff, metal wheels, and Jackie gave a big whoop as something appeared in the floor beneath it.

"Hey, look at this. I think I've found a way into the mine!"

Chapter Eight

Tunnels and Tracks

Gappy and Llew ran over to join Jackie while Pru watched from her post by the door, a look of envy on her face. "I was going to search over there next," she called.

The boys helped Jackie push the cart farther back, and sure enough, set into the cement floor was what looked like a round, concrete manhole cover.

"This must be it!" Jackie squealed in an excited whisper. "Can you move it?"

The manhole cover had a hole in the middle of it, big enough to fit a round tool or a couple of fingers. Llew looked around and spied a metal bar with a hook on the end of it lying on a nearby shelf. He picked it up and inserted the hooked end into the hole. Then he tried to lift the cover, but it was too heavy.

"Oof," he panted after a couple of tries. "I'm not strong enough. See if you can move it, Gappy."

Gappy took hold of the metal bar and stood with his head bowed, eyes squinted shut, summoning his special strength from deep in his belly. Then he opened his eyes, took a deep breath, and pulled the bar upwards. The manhole cover shot up, taking him by surprise, and he almost dropped it on his foot as he turned sideways and lowered it down onto the floor beside the hole. He laid the bar on top of it.

"Wow!" exclaimed Llew and Jackie in unison.

Gappy grinned sheepishly. "Yeah, I guess I used a bit too much vampire strength there. I'm glad I didn't drop it on my foot. That would have been really painful."

Llew clapped him on the back. "Good job. I'm jealous."

"Are we gonna go down and explore?" Pru called from the front of the shed. She was not as amazed at Gappy's show of strength as the others were because she had seen it before.

Llew beckoned to her. "You might as well join us, Pru. Hopefully the men have finished whatever they were doing down there and won't be back tonight."

Jackie shone her flashlight down the hole. They could see a rocky floor a few feet below and a large wooden crate that the men probably stood on to get out of the hole again.

"I'll go first," Gappy volunteered. He felt that he should get first look, seeing as he was the one who had raised the man-hole cover.

He sat on the edge of the hole and lowered himself down onto the crate, then jumped down onto the rock floor. The others followed him one by one and found themselves in a small cave that had been hewn out of the rock. At the back of the cave was a low opening.

Pru shone her flashlight into it. "It's a tunnel."

"Here, I'll go first," Llew said. "Hand me your flashlight, Pru, so I can light the way."

"No, I want to go first," Pru argued. "I don't see why boys always think they have to take the lead."

"Testy, testy," Llew joked, putting up his hands in surrender in the face of Pru's fierceness. "Go ahead. Lead the way."

"All right then," said Pru. "You next, Jackie, and the boys can follow you. To *protect* us in case anyone comes after us," she finished with a grin at Llew. Gappy and Llew looked at each other and shrugged, then fell in behind the girls.

With Pru in the lead they walked along the tunnel by the light of the girls' flashlights. The walls were very rough with jagged pieces of rock sticking out all over the place. They had to be careful not to scrape themselves. The ground underfoot was better, but it was still quite uneven, and they had to be careful not to stub their toes or trip over numerous bumps.

"This tunnel's quite straight," Gappy commented over Llew's shoulder as they walked along behind the girls. "I think we're heading straight for the hill."

"I think so too," Llew answered, ducking under a low-hanging lump of rock just in time. "Whoa, I nearly cracked my head open."

Just then the tunnel ended at a rough wooden door made of planks. "Maybe this is the mine," Pru called back. "Shall I open the door?"

"Wait," Llew said, pushing past Jackie to stand beside Pru. He pressed his ear against the door and listened for a moment. "I don't hear anything. I think it's safe."

"Good," said Pru and grasped the door handle.

The door was not locked and opened easily. The tunnel continued on the other side, but this time it was twice as wide, and the roof was a little higher. Wires ran along one wall, presumably to power the light bulbs that hung from the ceiling here and there.

"Can we turn the lights on?" Jackie asked, looking around for a light switch.

Llew shook his head. "Better not. We don't know if anyone else is down here. Anyway, I don't see a switch to turn them on with."

"C'mon, let's go," Pru urged impatiently. "We've got the flashlights."

Gappy came up to walk next to her as she set off down the tunnel. After sloping downwards for a while, the tunnel suddenly opened out into a large cave, and they saw the entrances to three more tunnels in the rocky walls.

"Which way, Jackie?" Gappy asked. "You've got the map,

haven't you?"

Jackie gave a gasp and felt in one pocket of her jeans and then the other. "Oh, no," she wailed. "I left it at home!"

There was a chorus of moans.

"Jackie, you nincompoop!"

"Jackie, you didn't!"

"Jackie, how could you forget?"

Jackie hung her head. "I know. I'm sorry. I was going to put my jeans in the wash, so I took the map out of my pocket and put it in my dresser drawer. I didn't know I was going to be wearing them again in the middle of the night, did I?"

"What should we do then?" Pru asked, feeling disappointed but sorry for Jackie at the same time. The poor girl looked so guilty about forgetting the map. "Should we choose a tunnel and see where it takes us?"

"We can try, I guess," Llew answered, sounding doubtful, "but remember what the map's like? It's like a maze."

"Which one should we try?" Jackie asked, looking at the three entrances. Each one looked the same as the next.

Gappy walked over to the middle of the three. "I think it's this one."

"I think you're right," Jackie agreed.

The four children walked down the middle tunnel behind Gappy, but after a while they came to a junction where the tunnel split into two.

"Which way now, Jackie?" Gappy asked.

Jackie looked right and then left. "Umm . . ."

Llew huffed. "C'mon, Jackie. You're the one who drew the map. Don't you remember?"

"I don't know," Jackie said, sounding frustrated. "I'm trying but . . . I . . . I just can't."

Pru suddenly gave a huge yawn. "Well, *I* don't think we should go any farther. We'll get lost. We can come back tomorrow in the daytime with the map."

Llew nodded reluctantly. "I guess so."

"Sorry," Jackie mumbled to Gappy as they headed back the way they had come. "I guess I'm just not used to adventures, like you and Pru are."

"It's all right," Gappy assured her. "It's really late, and we're all tired anyway. We'll do better tomorrow." He yawned. He was actually secretly relieved to be heading home to bed, and by the looks of the enormous yawns of the others, so were they.

* * * * * * * * * * * * *

The next morning it was a very sleepy foursome who assembled around the breakfast table in their pajamas in response to repeated summonses from Aunt Joelle.

"My, we've got a lot of sleepy heads, haven't we?" she commented as she dished out plates of French toast covered in strawberries and syrup with a dollop of cream. "Anyone would think you'd been up half the night!"

"Mornin' all," Uncle Peregrine boomed, coming into the kitchen from outside. A smell of cows wafted in with him. "Really, Llewellyn and Jacquelina! Still in your pajamas? What kind of farm kids are you?"

Llew grimaced at his dad's hearty cheerfulness. "It's all right for you, Dad. You don't mind getting up at the crack of dawn, but I do." He let out a huge yawn.

"Cover your mouth, Llew," said his mother out of habit. "You'd better eat up and get dressed because your dad's got a surprise for you."

Uncle Peregrine nodded. "Yes. I thought we could spend the day at Mount Snowdon." He looked at Gappy and Pru. "No one should leave Wales without seeing it. It's three thousand, five hundred and sixty feet high and the tallest mountain in England and Wales. We can ride up to the summit on the

Mount Snowdon Railway and walk down again. Should be a nice day."

Gappy and Pru smiled politely, but Llew and Jackie looked glum. "Dad, do we have to go today?" Llew asked.

Uncle Peregrine poured himself a cup of tea. "Why the long faces? I haven't got to the surprise part yet."

The four children looked at one another. They had planned to explore the Penffordd Slate Mine of course.

"Don't keep them in suspense, Perry," Aunt Joelle urged.

Her husband laughed. "If this lot can stop yawning long enough, I'll tell them. You remember Tom Smith from last summer, don't you?"

Gappy sat up in his chair. "Yeah, he was the Group A Flying and Levitation teacher at Camp Widdershins. Tom's cool."

Uncle Peregrine took a sip of his tea. "Well, it just so happens he's been attending a course in Chester on the Welsh border. He's heading back to the States in a couple of days, but when he heard we lived not too far away, he gave me a call and I suggested he come for a visit. He's going to meet us at Mount Snowdon and spend the day with us. On our way down the mountain, I thought it would be nice if we took a little, uh, detour off the beaten track to a little place I know of and put in some flying practice. I'm sure you boys would like to show Tom the progress you've been making since you saw him last."

Llew cheered up at the mention of showing off his flying prowess to Tom. "Really? That would be great! Good idea, Dad."

Jackie and Pru nodded happily, no doubt hoping that they would get to go flying again too, as the boys' passengers.

Uncle Peregrine drained his teacup and put it in the sink. "You kids hurry up and finish your breakfast while I phone and make reservations for the railway."

He tried a few times to get a dial tone and then gave up.

"The phone keeps cutting out. We've been having trouble with the lines all week. Lend me your cell phone, will you, Joelle?"

Aunt Joelle dug her cell phone out of her handbag and handed it to her husband. He soon reached the Snowdon Mountain Railway and made reservations for eleven o'clock that morning.

"Come on, everyone, we'd better hurry," Jackie said as she wiped up the last bit of syrup with her French toast. "It takes about an hour to get there, and we still have to get dressed."

The others finished their breakfast quickly and ran upstairs to get ready while Aunt Joelle packed them a picnic lunch.

In no time at all, the children were back downstairs again, dressed in jeans and tee shirts. They had sweaters and jackets with them too, as it was only May and Llew had said it would be cold on top of the mountain. They piled into Uncle Peregrine's battered, old station wagon and waved goodbye to Aunt Joelle.

The road to Mount Snowdon wound through the pretty countryside, past mountain streams, and through little stone villages surrounded by the inevitable stone-walled pastures of sheep.

"I'll never get tired of this lovely scenery," Pru sighed happily, gazing out the window. "You're so lucky, Jackie and Llew."

"We have nice countryside in the States too," Gappy reminded her.

Pru unstuck her nose from the glass. "Yeah, but at home it doesn't feel all old-fashioned and . . . and . . . I dunno . . . quaint. And there's always a big city not far away with big supermarkets and malls and department stores."

"I *wish* we had a supermarket or a mall with a big department store near us," said Jackie from the front seat. "Do you want to take a turn in front, Pru? Then you can moon over the lovely Welsh scenery all you like."

"Okay," Pru said. "Thanks, Jackie."

After paying a toll of forty pence to cross a low bridge where a river flowed into the sea, Uncle Peregrine obligingly pulled off to the side of the road so that the girls could change places.

As they headed farther north, the land grew more mountainous, especially after they drove through a tiny stone village called Beddgelert and passed a sign pointing to the Sygun Copper Mine. The road continued on through hillsides of rhododendron and trees and passed two large lakes called Llyn Dinas and Llyn Gwynant. Uncle Peregrine's old station wagon was beginning to feel the grade now as the road rose steeply. After a while they began to see less and less trees and bushes and more open, steep grassland with rocky slopes and outcroppings. Gappy and Pru tried to make out which mountain was Mount Snowdon.

"I think it's that one," Gappy pointed. "It looks the tallest."

"You're right," Uncle Peregrine said as they turned left and started driving up another steep road. He pointed out a signpost and parking lot to the left. "See there? That's one of the trails you can take up Mount Snowdon."

After another five miles of driving between mountains and along a narrow valley, they began to see signs for the Snowdon Mountain Railway. Finally they passed a terraced, slate-covered hillside on their right and entered the town of Llanberis. Uncle Peregrine drove past a large country-house-type hotel and turned right into a parking lot across from a little train station.

"Here we are," he announced as they got out of the car and stretched their legs. "Now, does anyone see Tom? I've never met him, so I don't know what he looks like."

Llew pointed to a tall young man with a spiky, black crew cut, who was walking toward them from a nearby car. "There he is. Hi, Tom!"

Tom Smith came up to them, grinning all over his handsome face. "Hi, you guys. Nice to see you again. How're you doing, Llew, Gappy? Hi, Jackie and Pru. Keeping the boys in line, I hope?"

He stuck out his hand to Uncle Peregrine. "And you must be Perry Abernathy. Pleased to meet you."

Uncle Peregrine shook hands. "How do you do, Tom? Llew and Jackie speak very highly of you, so I'm glad you could spend the day with us. Got your walking shoes on, I see."

Tom looked down at his feet where his jeans were tucked into brown hiking boots. "Yup. Say, this is gonna be fun, hey kids? Gappy, I hope you and Llew have been practicing your flying."

Gappy nodded. "Yes we have, Tom, and we're getting pretty good at it too. We've even taken Jackie and Pru flying with us."

"You have?" Uncle Peregrine looked surprised. "When?"

"The other day at the pond," Jackie told him. "It was really fun, wasn't it, Pru?"

Pru nodded. "Yeah, I can't wait to do it again."

"Hmm, I'll have to have a demonstration, won't I?" said Tom, shouldering a backpack. "I brought some goodies along with me."

"Me too," said Uncle Peregrine, hefting his own backpack. "We'd better get going. The train leaves in five minutes."

The little party crossed the street to the station, and Uncle Peregrine picked up their tickets from the ticket office. The tiny train was packed, but they managed to cram themselves into the last car. The compartments were narrow with two bench seats facing each other. Four people could fit onto one seat. None of the children or adults was really fat, but even so, it was a tight squeeze.

With a toot of its whistle the train began clanking up the

mountain on a narrow track, pushed from the back by its locomotive.

"Ooh, I hope we don't start sliding backwards," said Pru, looking out the window at the steep ascent.

"Don't worry," Uncle Peregrine assured her. "This is what's known as a rack-and-pinion railway. The track has bars running down the middle with deep teeth cut into them, and the train has cog wheels underneath, which grip the teeth to stop us falling backwards."

As the train chugged steadily upwards, they passed a high waterfall, and the sparse trees gave way to grassy slopes. Uncle Peregrine pointed out the first appearance of the peak. Every so often they passed small, stone ruins. The broken stone outlines were all that remained of the homes of people who used to labor in the slate quarries long ago, keeping a few animals too to help make ends meet. Here and there modern houses and farms nestled in the green valleys below.

Pru could not get enough of the scenery. "I wish I lived here," she said over and over again. "I'd live right down there in that green valley next to that lake and never leave."

"You'd get hungry pretty quickly, then," Llew told her.

Soon they passed a little cafe at the halfway point, and the grassy slopes gave way to a more rocky landscape as the train entered the appropriately-named Rocky Valley. It passed by tiny Clogwyn Station – the stopping point when ice and snow conditions made it too dangerous to continue – and then began curving around a sheer rock face.

"That's the Llanberis Pass down there to the left," Uncle Peregrine told them as the train chugged along an open stretch. "When the railway was first built, it had open-topped carriages, and the passengers would stand up to get a better look at the Pass. If it was breezy, many of them lost their hats, and so the valley became known as Cwm Hetia – Hat Valley."

As they approached the summit, the train began climbing the steepest slope yet. Uncle Peregrine pointed out the huge Dinorwig quarry where nearly three thousand men and boys had hewn ninety thousand tons of slate from the mountainside each year.

"It was a very hard life," he told them. "The average life expectancy for a quarry man was only thirty-seven years."

As the train traveled the final stretch to the summit, the rail embankment grew more narrow with a sheer drop on either side. They slowly clanked up the last few feet and came to a stop beside a concrete platform. Everyone piled out, enjoying a sense of freedom after being crammed together for the hour-long train ride. They followed the crowd of train passengers into a square building, which bustled with people toting rucksacks and metal walking sticks.

Llew nudged Gappy. "Those are the serious walkers," he said. "Not like us."

On the other side of the building was a door to the outside, and they went through it and began walking up a short slope to the summit. For the last few feet, a stone spiral staircase led to the very top of the mountain, and they climbed up one at a time to take turns standing on the actual summit.

The wind blew fiercely at the top, and it was biting cold. Pru did not like it much. She stood there just long enough for Tom to take a picture of her on his cell phone then scurried back down again. Shivering, she yanked a pair of gloves from her pockets and pulled the hood of her jacket over her red hair.

"Brrrr," she shivered. "The wind's so cold, and it was trying to blow me off the top. It made me dizzy. There's not much to hold onto up there, and I felt like I was going to fall off."

Tom smiled at her. "Well, you're safely on solid ground again, Pru. For now at least. Enjoy it while you can because I'm sure the walking trail goes steeply downhill most of the way."

Chapter Nine

More Flying Practice

After everyone had had a turn on the summit, they began walking down a trail, following a group of teenagers dressed in blue parkas and yellow hats.

"Must be a group from somewhere," Jackie commented. "Dad, which way are we going?"

Uncle Peregrine pointed down the path. "The trail continues on down there, or one can turn right and climb down a steep, rocky staircase. We're going to keep to the trail for a while though, and then we'll leave it and find the hidden place I told you about."

The four children followed behind Tom and Uncle Peregrine. Gappy would have liked to have spent more time enjoying the scenery, but the going was so rocky and steep that he simply had to watch where he was placing his feet.

After about half an hour Uncle Peregrine pointed to a huge outcropping of rock that bulged out of the hill to the right of the trail. He looked all around to see if any other walkers were in sight then touched Gappy's arm. "See that huge bulge of rock over there? I want you to run up the hill and go behind it. We'll follow you one by one, making sure no one sees us. We'll meet up behind the rock, and then I'll show you where to go next."

Uncle Peregrine looked around again to make sure the coast was clear. "Okay. Go for it!"

Gappy took off up the rocky slope as fast as he could, dodging around boulders large and small. He finally reached the big rock and went around it to the back side where he found a small, flat area of scrubby grass at the top of a rock-strewn slope. He sat down with his back against the rock to wait for the others and was soon joined by Pru. She flung herself down onto the grass next to him. "This is exciting, don't you think, Gappy?"

Gappy nodded. "Yes. I love it up here in the mountains – all open and windswept. Wait 'til the kids at school hear that we walked down the highest mountain in Wales."

"Maybe we'll fly down some of the way too," Pru said, chewing on a stalk of grass. "I'm sure Tom will be impressed at how much you and Llew have improved."

One by one the others joined them behind the rock. It was becoming a tight squeeze on the little patch of grass.

"Right," said Uncle Peregrine, who had arrived last. "Follow me."

He led the way past the rock and down the slope. Everyone began slipping and sliding because it was so steep.

"I hope we don't have to come back this way," Jackie panted as she landed on her butt for the second time. "Ow, that stone hurt!"

At the bottom of the slope stood another huge outcropping of rock. Uncle Peregrine paused for the others to catch up. "We're going to edge our way around this rock. Now, the path is very narrow, so be very careful not to fall over the edge. Especially you, Jackie and Pru. Maybe you should hold onto me and Tom."

Jackie grabbed the back of her dad's belt, and Pru held onto Tom's as they edged around the back of the rock. The ground fell away very steeply from the flat ridge on which they found themselves.

"Careful now," Uncle Peregrine warned again as Tom and the children followed him single file along the rocky ledge.

"Don't look down, Jackie," Pru called to her. "It'll make you dizzy." She clutched Tom's belt tightly and concentrated on watching her feet, so as not to trip.

The narrow ledge went on for quite a long way, and Gappy was just wishing they could get where they were going when Uncle Peregrine called back down the line.

"Just a little farther."

Sure enough, after a few feet he and Jackie disappeared around a corner, and when the others followed, they found themselves at the top of another grassy slope. At the bottom of it was a small, flat area of grass and then the sheer edge of the mountainside.

Uncle Peregrine pointed. "We go down there. It's not far now, but be careful. It's steep." He led the little party, slipping and sliding again, down the steep hillside to the bottom where it flattened out.

Gappy flung himself down on the grass. "Oh, it feels good to be on something wide and flat for a change."

"Time for some lunch, I think," Uncle Peregrine announced, putting his backpack down and opening it. "Let's see what we've got here. Oh, good, they're labeled. Ham and mustard, egg salad, and cheese and cucumber. That should hit the spot."

"Ooh, and there's pieces of cake too," Llew said, peering into the rucksack. "Good old Mom."

"And I've got some fruit and some bags of chips," said Tom, rummaging in his own backpack. "I never saw so many flavors of chips before. Oh, I guess I should say *crisps*, shouldn't I, now that I'm in the U.K.? Anyway, there's roast beef and Yorkshire pudding flavor, tomato, chicken, shrimp, and spring onion."

"Shrimp!" Pru exclaimed. "Eeuuww, I don't like fish."

"Yummy," Llew said in approval. "I'll have one, please,

Tom. I like to eat them at the same time as my sandwich."

Uncle Peregrine handed around juice cartons too, and there was silence for a while as everyone ate their lunch.

Afterwards Pru flicked away some crumbs and stretched lazily, a happy look on her face. "I'm ready for a nap now." By the looks of the others, they all felt the same way, but they helped Uncle Peregrine collect up the sandwich wrappers and juice cartons, which he stowed in his backpack.

"Anyone want an apple," asked Tom, but no one did. "Shall we do a spot of flying, then?" he suggested.

Gappy looked around. "Where? Here? Can anyone see us?"

Uncle Peregrine shook his head. "No. We're sheltered in this spot from the summit up above, the road down below, and the walking paths that lead down the mountain. No one can see us unless they decide to explore off the trails and do a bit of tough mountain climbing. Just be careful not to go any higher than that tall rock at the top of the slope because then you'll be visible."

"So, let's see your stuff, boys," Tom said.

"Yes, I want to see this too," said Uncle Peregrine, settling himself on the grass and leaning back on his elbows.

Gappy and Llew stood up. Gappy felt a little self-conscious with everyone staring at him waiting for him to perform, but he tried to ignore them and closed his eyes for a moment to concentrate.

After a few seconds the familiar surging sensation swept through his body, and he felt a faint pop inside his head as if a bubble had burst. He surged upwards, imagining air whooshing out of the soles of his shoes, turning him into Gappy the Rocket Man.

He shot upwards a few feet then forced himself to slow down and floated steadily higher until he was about fifty feet in the air. He hovered there for a moment looking down at the others far below. They were all gazing up at him, their hands shielding their eyes from the sun. He waved to them and slowly turned around in the air as Llew came shooting up to join him.

"Ready for a little display?" Llew called to Gappy as he hovered nearby.

Gappy nodded. "Sure. Follow me."

He leaned his body forward in the air, spread his arms wide like an airplane, and zoomed around in a couple of big circles, getting lower as he turned until he was about thirty feet above the flat, grassy field. Then he bent over, tilted his body headfirst, and zoomed downwards at an angle. Just before he reached a startled Tom, he righted himself in the air and landed gently on his feet in the grass.

Everyone clapped.

"Bravo, Gappy! Bravo!" Tom yelled in surprise. "I didn't know you were that good! My, you've come a long way since camp last summer."

Llew zoomed down just then but did not manage to quite right himself before he landed. He hit the grass at an awkward angle and sprawled flat on his face, knocking the wind out of himself.

Jackie ran over to him. "Llew, are you all right?"

Her brother rolled around on the grass for a moment clutching his stomach, his mouth open like a fish out of water. "Give me a minute," he wheezed faintly.

The others watched anxiously until he began to breathe better and was able to sit up.

He looked around at all their anxious faces. "I'm okay," he told them. "I forgot I'm not as good as Gappy yet. I should have gone slower and left more time to turn myself the right way before I landed."

Tom clapped him on the back. "Well, I think you did great, Llew. When you come back to Camp Widdershins, we're going to have to put you both in the advanced group."

"Yes, well done, boys," agreed Uncle Peregrine.

"I came here ready to give you some pointers," said Tom, "but I see you've worked out the techniques for yourselves. What else can you do?"

"They can take us for a ride," said Jackie and Pru at the same time.

Gappy dug an apple out of Tom's backpack. "Yeah, we can. And something weird happened, Tom, when I was flying around with Pru the other day. After a while, when I was starting to get the hang of it, it was like she suddenly stopped weighing anything, and I could lie forward in the air more and even hold her with just one arm."

"Yeah, it was cool," Jackie added. "It was like that for Llew too. It was pretty scary letting go at first though. I was sure I was going to go splat in the pond that we were flying over. Either there was some vampire stuff going on, or Llew's really, really strong, because he managed to hold my entire weight with one arm."

Tom munched on some grapes from his backpack. "You're right. That's what happens. When you first started flying with passengers, you probably felt a little nervous and tense, didn't you, boys? Because you were trying something new and weren't too sure if you could handle it?"

Gappy and Llew both nodded.

Tom spat out some grape seeds. "Well, when you feel that way, it makes your vampire energy get all balled up inside you. But when you start to relax and grow more confident, that tight bundle of energy relaxes too, allowing it to flow around your body. When that happens, little bits of it can escape and flow into the person you're flying with. That's why it started to feel as if Pru and Jackie didn't weigh anything, and why you were able to hold them with only one arm."

The girls' eyes were open wide. "So you mean Pru and I sort of became able to fly too? Ourselves?" Jackie shrieked.

Tom laughed at her excitement. "Well, only when the boys were holding you. But yes, for a while you too had a little bit of vampire energy in you."

"Cool," said Pru. "It was such fun being weightless, like I was in outer space or something. Of course, when we hit the ground, all my weight came back again."

Jackie jumped up. "Are you recovered now, Llew? Can you take me flying?"

Llew opened one eye as he lay on his side listening to the conversation. He squinted up at his sister's eager face. "I guess so. Can I have a drink first, Dad?"

Uncle Peregrine threw him a juice box. "See, it's not so tough being a vampire sometimes, is it, kids? Especially when you get to do things like flying?"

Llew drained his juice box. "I've never seen *you* fly, Dad."

His father smiled. "That's true. I don't do much flying anymore. Doesn't seem like there's much call for it, though I guess I could flit over to the cow barn instead of walking. Or I could herd the sheep from the air instead of using Dilys to do it. Boy, wouldn't they be surprised? I'd forgotten how much fun it was until I watched you boys zooming about up there. Now I'm thinking your mom and I are overdue for a bit of flying ourselves."

"When I was young," Uncle Peregrine continued, "I often used to take her flying – uh, once she got used to the idea of me being a vampire, of course. In fact, that's one of the ways I persuaded her to believe me when I first told her I was one. I thought she was going to have me admitted to the loony bin when I first told her. I had to show her some tricks so she'd see I was telling the truth."

"What happened then, Dad?" Jackie asked, looking interested.

"Well, she freaked out and almost brained me with a frying pan because she got such a shock when I levitated right in front of her and flapped around the living room. But then I accidentally bashed my head on the ceiling light and almost knocked myself out. I crashed down onto the carpet, and she was all worried and kissing me and telling me she loved me. Then when she saw I was all right, she started thinking that *she* must be going crazy, having hallucinations, and whatnot.

"Anyway, eventually she got used to the idea that her boyfriend truly was a real, live vampire, and then of course she had to be sworn to secrecy by the Vampire Council. Now she's married to me and has a vampire son, so . . ."

Llew shook his head. "You know, Dad, I can't believe I never thought to ask you how you first told Mom you were a vampire. I guess I always took it for granted."

Tom stood up and stretched, brushing grass from his jeans. "Well, I'd like to see you boys do some flying with the girls. And then we'd better think about getting off this mountain, don't you think, Perry?"

"Yes," said Uncle Peregrine. "We can either go back the way we came . . ."

He paused as the children groaned in unison, ". . . or we can fly down a good part of the way. We'd keep to this valley, then fly through a narrow pass and along another short valley, then walk through a storm drain to the next valley where we can pick up the main trail again."

"Is it safe?" Tom asked, looking over his shoulder as if he expected to see a hiker or two.

"A person would have to do some pretty tough climbing to get to a spot where they'd be able to see the parts we'll be flying in," Uncle Peregrine told him. "We'd better keep a sharp lookout, though. If anyone does spot us, we'll have to stop and do a bit of memory scrubbing. I don't like to do that, but . . . no, there's not much risk."

"I vote we fly, then," said Gappy. "C'mon Pru. Let's do a little demonstration."

Pru scrambled readily to her feet and came and stood on Gappy's feet with her back to him, holding him around his waist with her arms behind her back. He put his arms around her in turn, closed his eyes for a moment, and then began floating upwards. Even before he got more than a few feet into the air, Pru began to feel lighter to him, and he imagined he could feel the light, swooshy energy surging through his body and trickling through his fingers into her.

"Do you feel it?" he said into Pru's ear, then puffed at a tuft of hair from her ponytail that had gotten into his mouth.

Pru nodded. "Yeah, it's awesome! I feel so free, like I don't weigh *any*thing!"

She let go of Gappy and spread her arms wide. "Let's go flying!"

By this time they had risen to about twenty feet off the ground. Gappy leaned forward in the air with one arm around Pru's waist, stuck his other arm out to the side, and zoomed across the field in a zigzag pattern.

Llew and Jackie flew past just then. Jackie was shrieking in delight and egging her brother on.

"Faster, Llew! Faster!"

Llew obliged by leaning forward in the air to make himself more aerodynamic. Unfortunately he overdid it and Jackie shrieked again, this time in fear, as they both almost turned upside down. Llew wobbled a little in the air, coming dangerously close to the grass of the field, but managed to right himself just in time. He zoomed back up into the air with Jackie, then slowed down and flew a few lazy circles above the field.

"You'll just have to be satisfied with this, Jackie," Gappy

heard Llew yell to her as they flew nearby.

"Sorry, Llew," Jackie called back, sounding a little subdued after the fright of almost crashing down onto the field on her head. "I forgot you're still new at this 'cause you fly so well now."

After a few more passes over the field, Llew and Jackie landed in one piece, and Gappy and Pru floated down a few seconds later.

Tom and Uncle Peregrine came over to them, shouldering their backpacks. Llew's father clapped him on the back. "Very good, son. But, Jackie, don't push him so hard. He's not a horse."

Jackie looked shamefaced but then had to burst into giggles at the idea of Llew as a horse. "I know, Dad. I already said sorry to him."

Pru grabbed Tom's arm. "So, what did you think, Tom? Pretty awesome, huh?"

Tom smiled at Pru, whose green eyes were shining with excitement. Some of her wiry, red hair had come loose from her ponytail and was curling madly around her freckled face.

"Hey, Pru, you look cute with your red hair all curly like that," Llew remarked.

Pru blushed.

"Llew!" Jackie exclaimed. "Since when do you think girls are cute? You never say *I'm* cute."

"Well," said Llew, looking embarrassed, "you're just my sister."

"*Just* your sister? *Just* your sister?" Jackie spluttered, throwing grass at him. "Do you think I'm cute, Gappy?"

"Oh, yeah," Gappy agreed hurriedly. "Very."

Jackie stuck out her tongue at her brother. "There. See?"

Someone cleared his throat noisily nearby. "Uh, hmm, children? Cute or not, we'd better get moving," said Uncle Peregrine. "Joelle and I have tickets to a big fundraising event this evening."

"Right," said Tom. "How shall we do this? Are the boys going to take Jackie and Pru, or should they ride with you and I, Perry?"

"Ooh, I want to ride with you, Tom," said Pru at once. She shot an apologetic glance at Gappy. "No offense, Gappy."

Gappy grinned. "That's fine by me. It'll be nice flying by myself without getting a mouthful of your ponytail every other minute."

"I'll go with you, Dad," Jackie announced, "seeing as Llew's *just* my brother."

Llew made a face at her. "Good. Dad can take a turn at being the horse. Don't let her kick you, Dad."

"Pru, you don't have to stand on my feet with your back to me," Tom told her. "Just stand next to me with your arm around me, and I'll do the same."

Pru did as she was told. Then Tom put his right arm tightly around her and they rose up into the air. Almost immediately Pru could feel the weightless feeling already flooding her body. But there again, Tom was a much more experienced flyer than Gappy was.

Uncle Peregrine, on the other hand, seemed to be having a more difficult time getting off the ground.

"Bear with me. I'm a little rusty," he told Jackie as he wobbled up a few feet, leaving her behind on the ground. He shot up a few more feet, flew a couple of quick circles above her head, then floated back down again. "Okay, I've worked the kinks out. Ready?"

Jackie nodded doubtfully as she put her arm around him. "You're not going to drop me, are you, Dad?"

Her father laughed. "I'll try my best not to. No, really. It's like riding a bike. Once you learn it, you never forget." He tightened his arm around her, and they shot up into the air to join Tom and Pru, who were hovering overhead. Gappy and Llew flew over to them. Then, with Uncle Peregrine taking the lead, they leaned forward in the air and swooped down into the valley below.

Chapter Ten

Down the Drain

All the children shrieked as they plunged downwards. Gappy felt a surge of panic as he suddenly found himself doubting his ability to fly. He had never been this high in the air before. The valley floor was hundreds of feet below.

Tom flew by just then with Pru. "Calm down, Gappy, you're doing great. Just relax and enjoy it. Try doing some gliding, like this." He stuck out his outside arm, and Pru did the same. They began gliding gracefully like a bird on an air current.

Gappy tried to relax. He leaned more forward until he was lying on his stomach in the air, spread his arms wide, and glided after Tom and Pru.

"That's it," Tom called as Gappy caught up to them.

"Yippee!" Gappy yelled as he put on some speed and overtook them. He rocked his body to one side and turned the corner like an airplane. Then he tilted his body back and turned the other way.

"Show off," his uncle panted as Gappy zipped by him. Uncle Peregrine seemed to be flying rather jerkily, clutching tightly onto his daughter, who looked as if she were wishing she had stuck with Llew. Beads of sweat ran down his forehead as he rummaged in a pocket for his handkerchief.

"Dad!" Jackie shrieked as her father wobbled violently in the air.

"Sorry," Uncle Peregrine apologized, mopping his forehead. He wobbled again as he rammed the hanky back into his pocket. "Still rusty, I guess."

Tom heard him and flew closer to give him some tips to improve his technique. Uncle Peregrine listened gratefully, and Jackie heaved a sigh of relief as her father's flying leveled out and became a lot smoother.

Down and down they flew, and then they began flying along the middle of a long valley toward a narrow cleft in the rocks.

"That's the pass," Uncle Peregrine yelled.

As they came closer to the end of the valley, the walls began closing in around them, and everyone fell into single file behind Uncle Peregrine as they flew along the narrow pass. It opened out at the end into another small valley, and they flew on until they reached the foot of a rocky mountain. Then they floated down to earth, landing next to the open end of a huge, round pipe.

"We have to walk along this storm drain now," said Uncle Peregrine as everyone gathered around him. "Luckily there's hardly any water flowing out, so it shouldn't be too difficult. I'll go first, then you kids, and then you, Tom, can bring up the rear. There's a couple of torches in my backpack for the girls. Will you get them, Gappy?"

"Torches?" Gappy repeated. He pictured Jackie and Pru walking through the huge pipe holding thick sticks with flaming knobs on the ends. "Won't that be dangerous?"

"He means flashlights," Llew said, laughing at Gappy's expression.

"Oh," Gappy said. "Duh." He rummaged in his uncle's backpack and brought out two flashlights, which he handed to Jackie and Pru.

Uncle Peregrine shifted the straps of his backpack a little and stepped into the tunnel, followed by Jackie, then Llew, then Pru, Gappy, and finally Tom. The beams from the girl's flashlights picked out the trickle of water running down the center of the pipe. As they walked next to it, the air was full of the sounds of their footsteps and breathing.

"How far does this pipe go, Uncle?" Gappy called after they had been walking for five minutes.

His voice echoed in the pipe. "*GO, go, go, go . . .*"

"About another five minutes," Uncle Peregrine called back.

"*MINUTES, 'inutes, 'inutes, 'inutes . . .*" went the echoes.

"BOING!" Tom's backpack, full of apples and bottles of water, bumped against the side of the pipe.

"*BOING, boing, 'oing, 'oing . . .*" repeated the echoes.

Pru squeaked in surprise.

"Sshhh!" hissed Llew a second later.

The echoes immediately had a field day with these new sounds.

"*EEK! SSHHH! Eek! Sshhh! Eek! Sshhh! Eek! Sshhh . . .*"

"Sorry," Tom called softly from the back of the line.

"*SORRY, sorry, 'orry, 'orry . . .*"

After that everyone kept silent, the only noise being the sound of their footsteps, which kept up a constant echoey, shuffling sound inside the pipe. The light at the beginning of the tunnel had faded behind them now, and they would have been in complete darkness if not for the girls' flashlights.

After a while they began to see a bright speck ahead of them. It grew slowly bigger as they approached it, and they realized it was daylight streaming in at the other end of the tunnel.

"Hooray!" Jackie yelped, forgetting about the echoes. But they were not too bad, now that they were almost at the end of the pipe.

Uncle Peregrine halted just before they exited the storm drain. "I'll just have a quick look," he told them. "See that no one's about."

He stuck his head out and looked around. "Okay. I don't

see anyone. Quickly, now."

He walked out of the pipe, followed by the others. They found themselves halfway down a grassy hillside, the entrance to the storm drain looming blackly behind them.

"Now," said Uncle Peregrine, "we go up this hillside here, cross the train track, and pick up the trail down the mountain."

"Anyone want an apple or a drink?" Tom asked as they scrambled up the slope. Everyone did. They crossed the train track and sat down on some boulders next to the trail, and Tom handed out tart green apples and paper cups of water, which he filled from his water bottles.

Pru suddenly had a fit of the giggles. "Wasn't it funny when Tom's backpack full of apples and water bottles hit the side of the pipe?"

"Boing!" Llew boomed.

"Eek!" "Sshhh!" Jackie and Gappy squeaked and hissed at the same time.

Pru's giggles were infectious, and Tom burst out into a loud chuckle, startling a couple of approaching hikers who looked curiously at the laughing group. This only made everyone laugh even harder.

"Mad. Quite mad," Uncle Peregrine informed the couple as they walked by.

For the next hour, he led his group down the mountain trail. They tried to keep to the grassy edges whenever they could because in places the trail merely consisted of a slope of scree – loose stones – that made for quite precarious, slippy-slidy going.

At last they reached a steep, paved road at the bottom and walked down it to the main road.

"Well, that was a fun time," Tom said when they reached the parking lot. He emptied apple cores and empty water bottles into a convenient garbage can, then shook Uncle Peregrine's hand. "Thanks for asking me along, Perry."

"Thank you for joining us, Tom," said Uncle Peregrine. "Any time you're back in the U.K., look us up, won't you?"

"Sure," Tom answered. He grinned around at the children. "Nice seeing you all again. I'll see you at Camp Widdershins this summer, won't I?"

Gappy nodded. "You bet. And Pru can come this time, now that she's a vampire protector."

"Llew and Jackie might be able to join you too," Uncle Peregrine put in, "instead of going to camp in England."

The twins gazed at him in delight. "Really, Dad!"

Tom clapped the boys on the back and gave the girls a hug. "Fantastic. I'll see you soon then. Goodbye."

"Goodbye!" yelled everyone as Tom went to find his car.

"See you in the summer!"

"That was a lot of fun," said Gappy after they had all piled into the station wagon.

"It was," Uncle Peregrine agreed, putting the car in gear. "You boys are doing great at flying. As I said, I plan to take your Aunt Joelle for a spin in the near future. Won't she be surprised!"

Jackie giggled at the thought of her dad struggling to hold onto her plump mother as they flitted over the treetops.

"Did you really mean it when you said Jackie and I might join Gappy and Pru at Camp Widdershins this summer?" asked Llew.

"I did," said his father. "You had such fun last summer, your mother and I thought we'd go and visit your Uncle Burt and Aunt Livvie while you kids all went off to camp."

The four children grinned at one another in delight. That would be so cool!

Gappy and Llew fell asleep on the drive home, and Jackie and Pru chatted quietly to each other, not wanting to wake them. The boys were probably exhausted from their long flight down Mount Snowdon. And rightly so. By the looks of Uncle Peregrine's huge yawns, he was rather tired too, especially as it had been a long time since he had flown; and with a passenger as well.

"Would you mind staying on the road, Dad," Jackie blurted out with a squeal as the car drifted sideways, almost hitting a stone wall.

Her father rubbed his eyes hard and opened his window some more. "Sorry. It's getting warm in here, and I'm not used to so much exercise."

The rest of the journey passed uneventfully, and soon they were pulling into the driveway of Perryelle Cottage.

The boys woke up as the car came to a halt. "Oh, we're home," Gappy said, sitting up and stretching. "That was quick."

"Well, you've both been sleeping like babies the whole way home," Pru told him.

"Yeah, we had to put up with Llew's loud snoring, and grunting, and sighing, and far –"

"That's enough, Jackie," Llew interrupted, rolling onto her and clapping his hand over her mouth before she could say something unladylike.

"Mmmm, mmm," Jackie mumbled and took in a huge sniff of air through her nostrils.

Llew snatched his hand away, afraid that his irritating twin sister was about to blow her nose all over his hand.

Jackie sprang out of the car, laughing. "You never learn, do you Llew? I can always get a reaction from you."

"Yeah, you should ignore her, like I do with Pru," Gappy put in, getting out of his side of the car.

"What do you mean, ignore me?" Pru retorted at once.

"Children, children," Uncle Peregrine chimed in, interrupting their little spat. "We're all tired and hungry after our long day. I hope Joelle's got a nice tea ready for us."

At the mention of tea, the four children instantly stopped squabbling and grinned at one another sheepishly.

"You weren't really snoring," Jackie told Llew as they went into the house.

"And I'd never ignore you, Pru. You know that," said Gappy.

Pru grinned and linked arms with him as they followed the others into the big farm kitchen. "I know. You'd never get away with it, that's why."

Soon everyone was sitting around the big wooden table, drinking chicken noodle soup with crackers and cheese. Gappy and Pru eyed the laden table with approval – homemade quiche, salad, celery sticks to dip into salt before crunching, and little, round pork pies.

"What are those?" Pru asked pointing to a plate of round, brown balls covered in bread crumbs.

"Scotch eggs," Jackie told her. "They're hard-boiled eggs inside a sort of breadcrumby coating."

For dessert Aunt Joelle had made some gingerbread and a huge fruit salad with cream to pour over the top. The children tucked in hungrily as they told her all about the day's happenings.

Uncle Peregrine dug in as well, though he only ate a little because he and Aunt Joelle would be eating at the fundraiser. He winked secretly at the children as the boys described the progress they had been making with their flying. The four winked back at him and did not mention Uncle Peregrine's plans to take his wife out for a spin in the air. Luckily, at that moment Aunt Joelle was busy taking some lemonade out of the fridge, so she missed the flurry of winks.

Uncle Peregrine finished his last mouthful of fruit salad and wiped his mouth with his napkin. "Are we still giving the

Stewarts a ride to the meeting tonight, Elly?"

"I don't know if they still need us," said Aunt Joelle, smiling as the children got up to clear the table. "Their car might be fixed by now. Why don't you give them a ring?"

Uncle Peregrine picked up the wall phone nearby but put it back after jiggling the receiver up and down. "Not fixed yet. The dial tone's still going in and out. I wish the phone company would hurry up and fix the lines. A lot of the village is affected."

Aunt Joelle handed him her cell phone, and Uncle Peregrine made the call. He handed the phone back afterwards. "Yes, their car's still in the shop. I told them we'd pick them up at six-thirty."

Aunt Joelle nodded. "Well, kids, we'll be out late. Will you be all right by yourselves, or should I get Mrs. Slocum from the village to come and sit with you?"

Llew snorted. "We're too old for babysitters, Mom. We'll be fine."

His mother laughed and went to get ready to go out.

After Gappy and the others had finished loading the dishwasher, they went into the living room.

Jackie threw herself down in an easy chair. "What should we do this evening? Any good shows on TV, Llew?"

"I thought we were going to do some more exploring at the mine," said Gappy.

Jackie sat up. "Oh, yeah! How could I forget? Shows you I'm not used to this adventure business."

"This is the perfect time to do it," said Llew. "Mom and Dad will be out late, so we'll have a good amount of time to snoop around. Er, as long as someone remembers to bring the map this time," he added, with his nose in the air.

Jackie swatted him with a cushion.

"Ooh, it's exciting," Pru squealed. "I wonder what we'll find down there."

Gappy started to answer, but just then Aunt Joelle came in.

"We're leaving now," she told them. "Play some games or watch television, and go to bed at a reasonable time, won't you?"

"Have a good time, Mom," said Llew, evading the question.

Gappy felt a little uncomfortable about their secret night outing, since he had promised his mother he would not seek out any adventures while he was away. He soothed his conscience by telling himself that he did not know what Trevor and his friend Rhys were up to at the mine. Maybe they were just exploring too and not doing any harm. If he found out that the men were up to something bad, however, he would make the others come home and tell the grownups.

"Why the serious face, Gappy?" Jackie asked.

"You're not getting cold feet, are you?" said Llew.

Gappy shook his head as he heard the front door slam behind his departing aunt and uncle. "I was just feeling a bit guilty about this adventure we're going on when I promised my mom I wouldn't."

Llew stood up. "Well, if we find anything that looks dangerous, we'll come back and tell my folks, okay?"

Pru jumped up and down impatiently. "Come on, then. What do we need for our advent . . . uh . . . I mean, *safe* little exploration?" she demanded, with a glance at Gappy.

"I'll bring the map, of course," Jackie announced, and stuck her tongue out at her brother.

"And I'll bring the flashlights . . . I mean *torches* for me and Jackie," Pru said. "And should we take some cookies, I mean *biscuits*, and a couple of water bottles too?"

Llew clapped her on the back. "We'll make a British girl out of you yet, Pru. It's nice to hear you speaking proper English for a change."

Pru tapped him on the head. "Silly."

"We should all take sweaters, jumpers, woollies, or pullovers," Gappy joined in with a grin at Llew. "It's cooling off outside, and the mine is a bit chilly too."

Chapter Eleven

———————————————

Aaahhh-chooo!

In a few minutes the four children were back downstairs. Jackie loaded up a small backpack with a sandwich bag full of peanuts, raisins and Coco Pebbles, a bar of chocolate, and a couple of plastic water bottles from the fridge. At Llew's questioning look, she pulled the map from her jeans pocket with a flourish and waved it at him.

Everyone had sweaters tied around their waists, and Pru added the two flashlights to Jackie's backpack. Then they went out the kitchen door and wheeled the bicycles out of the shed.

"I think we should cut across the fields 'til we're past Cade's house," said Llew. "We don't want to advertise to Trevor or anyone else that we're heading towards the mine, do we?"

The others shook their heads. Llew was right. They should be careful.

The girls followed behind as Gappy and Llew wheeled the bikes across the bumpy field. They were hidden from the road by a high hedge, so no one would be able to see them.

After a while Llew stopped walking. "I think we're past Cade's house now, and it's starting to get twilighty. It's probably safe to ride on the road."

"Look, there's a stile just up there where the hedge gives way to a stone wall," said Pru, pointing.

They continued on to the stile, and Llew climbed up the steps and sat on the top of it. Gappy handed up the bikes to him, and Llew lowered them gently to the ground on the other side. Soon everyone was over the stile and standing on the side of the road. Then Gappy and Llew mounted the bicycles, and the girls settled themselves on the uncomfortable rear luggage racks.

"I wish I'd thought to pad these racks with some old towels or cushions," Jackie complained as she tried to get herself comfortable. "The metal strips dig into my backside."

"Stop complaining," Llew told her over his shoulder. "You have to expect some discomfort in an adventure."

"That's all very well for *you* to say, Llew," Jackie argued. "You've got a fatter backside than I do. Plus you're sitting on a nice, cushy seat full of gel."

"Don't you two ever stop arguing?" Gappy called across to them. "I thought twins were supposed to get along."

"We do get along," Jackie called back. "Llew's just irritating sometimes."

"Speak for yourself," Llew said, always wanting to have the last word. "Wanna race, Gappy?" He began pumping hard on the pedals.

"Go for it, Gappy," Pru urged as Gappy started pumping his pedals too.

They soon entered the darker shadows of the woods. Although they could see quite well with their vampire eyesight, the boys automatically began pedaling a little slower as the darkness closed around them.

After a while they reached the other side and began silently coasting down the hill. They stayed on the edge of the road, keeping an eye out for Trevor and Rhys. At last Llew and Gappy slowed down and came to a stop by the big bushes near the shed.

Gappy pointed and the others nodded in the darkness. Rhys' rusty, brown car was again sticking out of the front of the shed building. They laid their bikes down on the ground behind the bushes, and then the four of them crept over to the shed. They listened for a while at the side of the entrance but did not hear anything.

"I'll take a quick look," whispered Gappy. "You stay here."

He slid into the shed and crouched next to the car, ready to dart out if he should hear the men coming, but all was silent. Trevor and Rhys must have gone down the manhole into the mine. Gappy walked around the car to the back of the shed. Sure enough the rusty cart had been pushed back to reveal the tunnel entrance. The round cover was now lying next to the black hole in the concrete floor.

Gappy knelt down and poked his head through the hole, but still heard no sound of the men. He got to his feet and went back to the entrance of the shed and beckoned the others in. "All clear."

The girls and Llew squeezed themselves past the car into the shed and joined Gappy by the hole in the floor. Gappy sat down on the edge of it and lowered himself down onto the crate. Then he jumped down into the cave. Pru and Jackie followed him, then Llew.

"I'll go first this time, if you don't mind," Gappy announced to Pru, who nodded graciously.

They walked single file down the uneven, rocky tunnel, the girls shining their flashlights ahead of them so that no one would scrape themselves on the jagged pieces of rock sticking out of the walls. When they reached the rough wooden door, Gappy pressed his ear against it.

"Don't hear anything," he told the others in a low voice. "Let's take a look at the map first before we go in."

Jackie took the map out of her pocket, and everyone crowded around to look at it. Pru obligingly shone her flashlight onto it so they could see the drawn lines more clearly.

Gappy traced a line with his finger. "Here's where we went the first time we were here."

"Yes, that's the cave there with the three tunnels leading off of it," said Pru. "We chose the middle one, remember?"

"That's right," said Gappy, brushing strands of Pru's red hair off the page. "Move your head out the way. I can't see."

Llew was craning his neck to see the map too. "I think we should try and find that big circle with the X in it. Seems like a big X would mean there's something important about that cave, or whatever it is."

Gappy nodded. "We should take the right-hand tunnel then. Then we turn left at this fork and right at the next fork. There's a few more turns and some small circles with small X's, and then farther along there's the big circle with the big X."

"Turn the flashlights off," Llew said, as Jackie folded the map and stuffed it in her pocket. "Just in case."

The girls switched off their flashlights, and Jackie let out a little squeal as they were plunged into pitch darkness.

Gappy fumbled for the door handle and slowly opened the door. Everyone held their breaths and listened.

"It's okay," Gappy hissed after a few seconds. "No one near."

Feeling around them like blind people, the girls and Llew followed Gappy through the doorway. The door swung closed behind them as silently as it had opened.

"Why don't they switch the lights on?" Pru whispered as they stood together in the pitch blackness. "Oh, do you think Trevor and Rhys are vampires?"

"I don't think so," Gappy answered.

"Me neither," said Llew. "If they were, I would have felt it, wouldn't you, Gappy? I can't describe it, but other vampires just feel different to me somehow."

Gappy nodded. "Yeah, like they give off this weird kind of vibration when you get close to them. It's funny, I never realized they did that until you said something, Llew."

"I hate being in the dark like this," Jackie complained. "I can't see my hand in front of my face. Maybe Trevor and Greasy Cap switch the lights off as they go, to save electricity or something. They might have a generator somewhere."

"It's good they don't have lights blaring though," said Pru. "It's safer to be in the dark where they can't see us."

"The thing is, when there's no light coming in from anywhere, *I* can't see, either," said Gappy. "Even with my vampire eyesight. You'd better turn the flashlights back on, but cover the lenses with your hands so they don't let out much light."

"Can we please get a move on?" Llew urged. "I'm feeling a bit claustrophobic, and the night's not getting any younger, you know."

"And miles to go before I sleep," Jackie added. "That's from a Robert Frost poem. We learned it at school. 'The woods are lovely, dark and deep, but I have promises to keep, and miles to go before I sleep, and miles to go before I sleep.' "

"That's all very nice, Jackie," said Llew, sounding irritated. "You can stay here and spout poetry if you like, but I'm heading off to explore."

"Hear, hear," Gappy agreed, shaking his head. "Girls!"

Jackie sniffed. "Sorry if I'm more educated than you are, Llew. Come on, then. You need me. I've got the map."

"What do you mean by 'girls', Gappy?" Pru retorted as they started off up the tunnel. "I'm a girl and I hate poetry . . . er, no offense, Jackie."

"That's all right," said Jackie. "I don't like it much either. That poem just stuck in my head for some reason."

"I was just teasing," said Gappy, "but sshhh, we'd better stop talking, or someone might hear us. Anyone would think we were on a school outing, the way everyone's jabbering. Follow me in single file. Keep your flashlights covered, and be prepared to turn them off if we hear anyone coming."

"Yes, *sir.*" Jackie snapped out a salute. "I feel like I'm in the army and you're the drill sergeant."

Everyone stopped talking after that and followed Gappy down the wide tunnel. It began sloping downwards, and they soon reached the large cave with the entrances to the three tunnels. The air was beginning to feel a little chilly by now, so they all stopped to put on their sweaters before entering the right-hand tunnel.

This tunnel was rather narrow, but the walls were smooth, so they did not have to worry about scraping themselves against jagged rocks. After walking for a while, they came to a fork and stopped to look at the map again.

"Left," Jackie said, pointing on the map. "Then right at the next fork."

"Right. I mean left," said Gappy as Jackie stuffed the map back in her pocket.

The left-hand tunnel was identical to the tunnel they had just left. Electric wires still ran along the wall with the occasional caged light bulb here and there.

"When we were here before, we could have just followed the wires," Pru remarked as she followed closely behind Gappy.

"Yeah, but I'm sure other tunnels have wires too," Gappy answered.

After turning right at the next fork and walking about one hundred feet, Gappy stopped suddenly. "I see a light. Better turn off your flashlights, girls."

Jackie and Pru did so, and the tunnel instantly became dark. But Gappy was right. There was a faint glow ahead.

"Quiet now, and be ready to run if we have to," he whispered over his shoulder, and Pru passed the message back to Jackie and Llew.

Keeping close to the wall, the four children crept up the tunnel. As the light grew brighter, they saw that the tunnel bent sharply to the left just beyond a large pile of rock. The roof of the tunnel had a gaping hole in it just there, and they eyed it nervously as they approached. However, the rest of the roof looked solid enough.

They edged past the rock fall and peered around the bend in the tunnel. A few feet away lay a huge slab of rock that looked as if it had fallen out of the left-hand wall, leaving a narrow alcove behind it. And just beyond the slab of rock was the entrance to a cave.

Gappy held up his hand to tell the others to stay back while he squeezed past the slab to take a look.

The cave was not very large and contained three folding lawn chairs and a card table. A couple of tattered paperbacks lay on the table with some sandwich wrappers and a half-empty bottle of Coke. The light came from a lantern that stood on a shelf of rock at one side of the cave.

Gappy was just turning to go back to the others to report what he had seen when he suddenly heard faint voices. Farther up the tunnel beyond the cave appeared a bright light.

Gappy quickly darted back to join the others, who had crouched down behind the slab as soon as they had seen the light.

The sound of footsteps approached. Gappy hoped that the bearer of the light was just returning to the cave. If he should walk past the slab of rock, he would surely see the children hiding there.

Luckily Gappy's prayers were answered. Two men appeared behind the flashlights they were carrying and entered the cave.

One of them let out a grunt of pain in what sounded like Trevor's voice. "Ouch! I really bashed my elbow back there, and now I just bumped it again on that stupid lump of rock sticking out."

"Yeah, I wish the electrics was working down 'ere," the

other man growled in Rhys' gravelly voice.

Gappy nodded to the others, and Llew gave him a thumbs-up. Good. At least they would not have to worry about the men turning on the lights.

"So, we've got three days left to prepare the recruits, huh?" said Trevor.

"Recruits? Yeah, that's a good word for 'em," Rhys chortled. "In-*voluntary* recruits, though. It's not like they had a chance to say no, did they?"

Trevor snickered. "They should appreciate what we're doing for them, that's what *I* say. I mean, there they were, sleepin' on the street, not knowin' where the next meal was comin' from, and now they're in a nice, dry cave, eating three meals a day . . ."

"Yeah, they eat better than *I* do," Rhys griped. "Don't know why they keep complaining. Fresh vegetables? Steak every night? I can only afford steak once a week, if I'm lucky."

"More like once a month," Trevor growled. "They'd better be in good shape for the ceremony, or Hillary Sleeth's not gonna be happy."

"So, what time is she arriving on Friday?"

"I think around midnight. She and Diggory Humbold are collecting Seymour Dusk from Cardiff airport on Friday afternoon . . ."

Gappy gave an almost silent gasp at the mention of Seymour Dusk. Mr. Dusk had been the Group B flying teacher at Camp Widdershins last summer and was in cahoots with the evil Master who was trying to bring back the Old Order of Vampires. On two occasions Gappy had been held prisoner while one or the other had tried to get him to join their movement.

Gappy and Pru looked wide-eyed at each other. To think that Seymour Dusk should be up to his usual tricks here, all the way across the Atlantic Ocean, in the very same village where Gappy's cousins lived. What were the odds of that?

". . . to their hotel in Dyffryn Ardudwy for supper," Trevor was saying. "Then they're going to meet up with Maddox at Harlech Castle – I guess there are secret dungeons down there that the tourists don't know about. Then they'll head on over here for the biting ceremony."

This time it was Jackie's turn to gasp, though it came out as a high-pitched squeak. Llew quickly put his hand over her mouth, and the children held their breaths, hoping Trevor and Rhys had not heard.

"Wawazat?" said Rhys, and there came the sound of a chair creaking under someone's weight.

"Relax. It's prob'ly a bat," Trevor told him. "There's tons of them in this mine, nasty things. It's getting late. They're get-ting ready to fly."

Gappy and the others heaved silent sighs of relief as the two men continued their conversation, unaware that four pairs of ears were listening to them just beyond the cave entrance.

"Why don't Hillary Sleeth stay here, Trev?" Rhys asked.

Trevor sighed. "I dunno. I guess the little village of Aber-gath ain't posh enough for 'em."

"Yeah, to go with their high and mighty names. Trev? What time's Maddox comin' to inspect the, uh, recruits tonight?"

"About eleven, eleven-thirty."

The men fell silent then, and Gappy heard one of them yawn.

Suddenly Llew felt a sneeze coming on. He immediately pressed a finger under his nose to try to stop it and retreated back around the corner into the other tunnel. As Jackie fol-lowed him to see what was the matter, Llew gulped frantically in a desperate attempt to stop the sneeze. But as he rounded the rock fall, he could hold it back no longer.

Aaahhh-chooo!

Gappy and Pru instantly froze and put up their hands.

"Aaahhh-chooo!" The sneeze exploded out of him, and the echoes instantly picked it up and threw it all around, making it sound as if a hundred people were sneezing – not just one young boy.

With a startled, "What the heck!" both men exploded out of the cave. A flashlight shone on the backs of Gappy and Pru as the two children turned to run around the bend in the tunnel to join the others.

"Stop right there!" Rhys shouted. "We've got guns and we'll shoot you if you don't stop."

Gappy and Pru instantly froze and put up their hands.

Chapter Twelve

Prisoners

Trevor and Rhys edged around the fallen stone slab, keeping their flashlights trained on Gappy and Pru. At the mention of guns, Pru had dropped her own flashlight and heard the lens break with a tinkle of glass.

One of the men grabbed the scared kids by the shoulder and roughly turned them around. Gappy and Pru were blinded by the beams of light shining in their faces, but they heard Trevor's voice exclaim in annoyance.

"Well, if it isn't two of those little brats from the village! How did you find the way in? Are the others with you?"

Gappy squinted into the light. "No. It's just us two."

Trevor grunted in disbelief.

I've got to try and stall them to give Jackie and Llew time to escape, Gappy thought to himself.

He lowered his arms and bent over double with a loud groan. "Oh, my stomach," he wailed. "I've got cramps."

"He's probably got appendicitis," Pru yelled, playing along. She lowered her arms too and shifted sideways, then bent over as if to help Gappy, giving Trevor very little room to pass by.

"Think I'm stupid?" Trevor snapped. He roughly pushed Pru out of the way and quickly strode past her to look in the other tunnel. He disappeared around the bend but returned a few seconds later.

"No sign of anyone," he told Rhys.

Gappy and Pru heaved secret sighs of relief.

The two men dragged their prisoners into the cave and

pushed them against the back wall. "Now, what you two busy-bodies doin' 'ere, interfering in things that are no business of yours?" growled Trevor.

"Yeah, how did you find this cave?" Rhys added.

"I dunno," Gappy answered with a sullen look on his face. He certainly was not going to say anything about the map. He shrugged. "Just lucky, I guess."

Rhys snorted. "Some luck! Trev, I think there's something more to him than meets the eye."

The flashlight wavered as Rhys approached Gappy and examined his face closely. Then he quickly aimed his gun at Pru. "I do believe this boy's a vampire."

Trevor lowered his flashlight. "How can you tell?"

Rhys snickered. "That's where I've got one up on you, Trev, though God knows why. You've been working for Hillary Sleeth longer than I have. No, it's this creepy kind of feeling I get whenever I'm close to a vampire. There's something about the eyes too. I'm hardly ever wrong."

Trevor pursed his lips and frowned. "Don't be so quick to gloat, Rhys. I'm still the one in charge here, remember? If he's a vampire, you're lucky he's still a young 'un, or else he'd have taken your head off already. Nah, he probably don't have many powers yet. Keep your gun aimed at his little friend, though. If he tries any funny business, shoot her."

Pru gasped as Rhys jabbed her in the ribs with his gun.

"What are your names?" Trevor demanded.

Gappy and Pru did not answer.

Rhys sighted down the barrel of his gun and pushed something down with his thumb. It made a clicking sound. Gappy thought it might be the safety catch.

"I'm Gappy and she's Pru," he said quickly.

"What are you doing down here?" Pru asked, trying to hide the quiver in her voice.

"How much did you hear?" Rhys said back at her.

"Nothing," answered Gappy and Pru together.

The men looked at each other.

Trevor nodded. "Uh, huh. Well, I'm afraid we're gonna have to keep you in suspense for now 'cause it's more than me life's worth to e-lab-or-ate, see?"

He moved closer to Pru, put a dirty finger under her chin, and jerked her head up.

"And guess what, Rhys? I think we just got ourselves another recruit."

Rhys snickered loudly, but kept his gun trained on Gappy's heart.

"What do you mean?" Gappy blurted out as Pru squealed in fright. "Recruit for what?"

Rhys giggled and gnashed his teeth in an overdramatic fashion. "Why, for the biting, my dears."

"That's enough, Rhys," Trevor growled. He gripped Pru's arm. "C'mon. We'll put this one in with the homeless folks. And you, you little snoop, can keep yourself company in your own private cell. I don't think Hillary Sleeth will want you mixing with the regs before she's had a chance to get at them herself."

"Take your hands off me," Pru yelled as Trevor tried to drag her from the cave. "Gappy!"

Gappy wildly tried to think of what he could do as Rhys grabbed hold of his arm as well and started pulling him toward the cave entrance.

We can't be separated from each other, he thought. *We just can't!*

He could feel his super strength bubbling under his skin, ready to lash out and throw Rhys against the wall. But the sight of Trevor's gun jammed into the small of Pru's back stopped him. He could not take the chance of being able to get rid of Rhys and reach Trevor in time before he shot Pru.

"You don't want Pru sharing a cell with the homeless peo-ple," he blurted out suddenly. "She's a vampire too."

Trevor paused at the cave entrance.

"No she ain't," Rhys jeered. "You just don't want to be sep-arated from your little girlfriend."

Pru looked back at Gappy, her eyes open wide. What was Gappy up to?

Gappy stared back at her while he shouted at Trevor. "It's true. She is a vampire, so you'd better keep us together."

He tried to ignore Rhys' gun jabbing into his ribs as he turned his gaze on Trevor. "You wouldn't want to get Hillary Sleeth all upset, would you?"

Rhys snorted. "C'mon, Trev. He's bluffing. She ain't no vampire."

But Trevor hesitated, looking back at Gappy with an un-certain look on his face.

"Prove it," he said.

"Pru, show them what you can do," Gappy shouted.

Pru gaped at him.

"Close your eyes and concentrate, Pru," Gappy urged, try-ing to communicate to her with his eyes that she should trust him.

Pru looked doubtful, but she obediently closed her eyes and stood with her head bowed.

Now that all of the men's attention was focused on Pru, Gappy closed his own eyes and began concentrating. He meant to try and make Pru levitate by using telekinesis. He had prac-ticed it over and over again and had progressed to moving big-ger and heavier things, such as a bag full of books and eventually even his desk. If he could just conjure up the same feeling that had flooded through his head when he had finally managed to move his solid, wooden desk with his mind, maybe he could move Pru too. Of course, people were quite different from inanimate objects like desks and book bags. They had emotions and electrical energy. Gappy hoped this would not affect the telekinesis.

Five seconds dragged by.

Pru stood stock still like a statue, her eyes closed, Trevor's gun still pressed into her back. She was probably thinking her best friend was crazy.

Another second went by.

"See? Told you she weren't no vampire," Rhys crowed. "He's just trying to delay things."

"Hey!" Trevor shouted in surprise as Pru suddenly floated up about four inches into the air.

Pru was even more startled than he was to find herself suddenly weightless and leaving the ground. However, she had to act like it was nothing unusual. She opened her eyes and gazed at Trevor. The gun in his hand was now drooping down to the floor.

"You see?" she managed, hoping her voice would not squeak and give her away. Although she was still very frightened, it was an awesome feeling to be hovering above the ground all by herself.

Gappy struggled to keep Pru in the air for at least a few seconds, but it was costing him a superhuman effort to do so. He would not be able to keep it up for much longer. The telekinesis was rapidly draining all of his energy, and he knew he was about to drop her at any moment.

He squeezed his eyes shut and managed to wring out one more ounce of energy. It was barely enough to float her gently back down, which was why Pru's feet hit the ground a little harder than Gappy intended.

And then he just could not help it – his breath exploded out of him in a monstrous, "Ffffooooosshh!"

As everyone jerked their heads his way, Gappy managed to

make the explosion appear to be a humongous sneeze like the one that had exploded out of Llew and landed him and Pru in this mess. Well, at least his cousins had been able to escape. He hoped they would soon be cycling home to get help.

Trevor grabbed Pru's arm again. "Okay, maybe you are a vampire. We'll put you two in together."

"But Trev," began Rhys, "I could have sworn –"

"Enough," Trevor snapped. "We're wastin' time. We'll put them in the far cell and be done with it. It don't matter now." And with a prod of his gun, he pushed Pru out of the cave, turned left, and marched her down the tunnel.

Rhys hurried to keep up, repeatedly jabbing Gappy in the ribs with his gun, as if to remind him who was boss. He kept up a constant muttering under his breath.

They reached a sharp bend in the tunnel, turned left, and saw a glow from a lantern up ahead. As they approached the lantern, there came a great hullabaloo of shouts and yells. The sound was coming from a big cave on their right, whose entrance was barricaded by a wall of metal bars. As they came level with the cave, a scrawny, unkempt man with a wispy beard began pulling against the bars of his prison like a madman. He opened his mouth wide in a snarl, revealing a gold front tooth that glinted in the light.

"Let us out! Let us out!" he yelled in a hoarse voice.

He was joined at the bars by two bedraggled women. One wore baggy, grey sweatpants, the other a tattered, blue dress. They both looked terrified.

"You've no right to keep us here!" screeched the woman in the blue dress.

The woman wearing the baggy sweatpants just held her head with both hands and moaned. "Aaiieee, aaiieeeeee."

"Why're you keeping us here," boomed a loud voice just then. A huge mountain of a man suddenly rushed at the bars and threw his weight against them. The bars rattled a little, but stood firm, and the man fell back with a cry, clutching his shoulder.

"Shut up!" Trevor yelled back loudly as he and Rhys hurried past with their captives. Gappy spied more prisoners huddled together at the back of the cave. They stared at him with sullen faces.

"Waaaaah!" a new voice suddenly wailed, full of misery. Pru automatically paused for a moment in shock. Was that a young child?

Trevor gave Pru an extra hard jab with his gun, as if to pay her back for almost tripping him.

As they stumbled down the tunnel, the cries of the prisoners faded behind them. Soon they took a turn to the right, and ahead of them, illuminated by the men's flashlights, was the entrance to another cave. It looked smaller than the last one but was fronted by the same barricade of solid-looking metal bars.

Trevor squished Pru against the wall as he reached up and took down a long, black key from a nail that had been hammered into the rock. Then he marched her over to a metal gate set into the wall of bars, inserted the key into the lock, and turned it. He kicked open the gate with his foot and shoved Pru into the cave.

Pru stumbled forward and almost fell. She recovered quickly and turned around to face the gate, just as Gappy cannoned into her with the help of a hefty shove from Rhys. Trevor promptly turned the key again, locking them in.

"Bet you wish you hadn't been so nosy now, don't you?" he sneered. "And don't think you can escape by using any vampire powers. These bars are made of steel. And, yeah, Rhys and I are also immune to telepathy. We work for vampires, so we're protected, see?"

Trevor suddenly hawked up a huge glob of spit and spat it between the bars of the cave. The glistening glob landed on the side wall and began trickling down.

"Urgh, why'm I wasting my breath?" he continued, wiping his mouth with the back of his hand. "You're only, what . . . ten . . . eleven years old? Your powers are still only baby ones, anyway."

"Aw, diddums," put in Rhys and sucked his thumb noisily.

The two men broke into fits of laughter and threw a few playful punches at each other. Then Rhys managed to connect with Trevor's sore elbow, at which point Trevor gave a yell and promptly boxed Rhys' ears.

"Ow, what you do that for?" Rhys yelped, dodging out the way.

Trevor nursed his elbow. "Clumsy fool. C'mon. Let's get out of here."

"Can't you leave us one of your flashlights?" Gappy called after them.

"If you're vampires, you don't need light," Trevor called back over his shoulder. He and Rhys disappeared around the bend.

As the light faded, Pru gave a little shriek and fumbled about, trying to find Gappy.

"It's all right," said Gappy, reaching out for her. "Wait 'til your eyes get used to it."

"It's all right for you to say. You've got vampire eyes," Pru snapped.

Gappy pulled her down to the ground to sit next to him. "Don't panic, Pru. There's some light coming in from the lantern in the other tunnel. There, you see? Thank goodness Llew and Jackie have escaped. They'll be able to bring help."

For a moment the two friends sat silently side by side, each wrapped in their own thoughts. Gappy whistled softly between his teeth. The old, familiar habit helped him think.

After a while, he began to chuckle.

"What can you possibly find funny enough to laugh about?" Pru demanded crossly.

"I was just remembering how I almost busted a gut making you float up off the ground."

Pru sighed. "I must admit it was pretty awesome. I thought you were crazy at first when you told me to show them I was a vampire. How did you do it?"

Gappy shifted his weight as a pebble dug into his leg. "Well, I guess I can tell you now because you've seen it. Mom and Dad told me to keep it a secret because I'm really too young to be able to do it yet, and bad people might try to force me to help them commit crimes if the word gets out."

Pru huffed impatiently. "Do what?"

"Telekinesis."

Pru gasped. "You mean, like moving things with your mind? Like *Carrie* in that Stephen King movie?"

"Yeah," said Gappy. "I only just learned how to do it a couple of weeks ago. I started out with a toy car, and then I kept practicing on bigger and bigger things. I even managed to move my desk a few inches. I didn't know if it would work on a person, especially a heavy lump like you –

"Ow! –

"– but it was the only thing I could think of. Otherwise Trevor and Rhys would have separated us."

Pru tried to get comfortable. "Well, I'm glad it worked. It did feel really awesome when I was, like, levitating all by myself, so I guess I'll forgive you for calling me a heavy lump."

Gappy rummaged in his pocket and brought out a half-melted bar of chocolate. He gave half of it to Pru, and they sat nibbling, trying to make it last. The taste and feel of melting chocolate in their mouths was comforting, especially now when they were sitting in gloomy darkness, feeling scared and lonely.

"What do you think's going to happen to those people in the cave?" Pru asked after a while. "Do you think it's something to do with the Old Order?"

Gappy nodded. "Yeah. I couldn't believe it when they said Mr. Dusk's name, could you? It's like I can't get away from him. Wherever I go, he goes. Even across the ocean. What're the chances of *that*?"

"I know," Pru agreed. "It does seem like too much of a co-incidence."

She shivered. "And what's a *biting* ceremony? It sounds scary."

"I don't know, but I can guess," said Gappy. "I think Mr. Dusk has been having trouble persuading vampires to join the Master's Old Order movement, so he's decided to create his own supporters. He's kidnapped a bunch of homeless regs that no one will miss, and he's going to bite them and turn them into vampires. That's probably what the biting ceremony's for. And some other vampires, who belong to the U.K. part of the Old Order –"

" – snooty Hillary Sleeth and snobby Diggory Humbold," Pru put in.

"Yeah, and that Maddox guy who was talking to Trevor and Rhys in Maisie's teashop – they're coming to help him. Maybe there's a limit to how many regs a vampire can bite in one night."

Pru shivered again and wrapped her arms tightly about herself. "It's so scary and horrible. Those poor people. They don't know what's in store for them. And what about that kid we heard, Gappy? Is he homeless too? He must be absolutely terrified."

Gappy put his arm around Pru. "I guess some kids *are* homeless. Maybe he belongs to one of the women."

"I bet Hillary Sleeth looks like Cruella De Vil in *The One Hundred and One Dalmatians*," Pru said. "Or the wicked Queen in *Snow White and the Seven Dwarfs*. You know, tall and bony with a really long, sharp face and long, sharp fingernails painted red."

"With thin, pointy, black eyebrows and thin, mean lips covered in bright red lipstick," Gappy added.

"Ooh, don't!" Pru squealed. "I can't bear it!"

She burrowed her head into Gappy's shoulder. "I'm really scared. What are we going to do?"

"I'm trying to think," said Gappy. "I wonder where Llew and Jackie are. I hope they haven't gotten lost."

Chapter Thirteen

Twins in Trouble

After the Big Sneeze explosion, Jackie and Llew quickly crouched down behind the rock fall, but then decided they should make a run for it in case the men came looking for them.

Llew took Jackie's hand to guide her in the dark tunnel, and they ran down it as fast as they could. Actually it was more like speed-walking because they were scared that the men would hear their sneakers pounding along the ground.

After what seemed like forever, they came to the end of the tunnel, and it was not a moment too soon. Just as they reached the bottom and turned left at the fork, Trevor entered the tunnel they had just left and walked down it a little way, shining his flashlight around.

Llew pushed Jackie into a narrow opening in the wall. It was just big enough to take them both, and they huddled inside as the end of the tunnel they had just left glowed from the light of Trevor's powerful flashlight.

"Please, oh, please don't come any farther," Jackie prayed under her breath as she peered over Llew's shoulder. Much to her relief the light began to fade as Trevor quickly gave up the search and turned to head back up the tunnel. As he turned the bend past the rock fall, the brother and sister were left in darkness again.

"Quick, let's take a look at the map and check that we were supposed to turn left there," Llew said in a low voice.

"I'm sure it *is* the left one," Jackie answered urgently. She was desperate to keep going in case Trevor decided to come back and search farther.

Llew, however, refused to budge until he had checked the map first. "If we're going to get help," he told his fidgeting sister, "we simply can't get lost."

Jackie jerked the map from her pocket and unfolded it, her fingers trembling. Llew took it from her as she switched her flashlight on. She took care to shield the beam with her hand so that there was just enough glow for them to make out the markings on the map. Llew was standing in the entrance to the alcove with his back to the tunnel so his body also shielded some of the light.

He checked the map quickly, running his finger over the lines. "Yes, we came the right way," he murmured. "There's a long, straight bit now, then we turn right at the next fork and left at the next one."

Jackie snatched the map back and stuffed it into her pocket. "Okay, right, left, and then we should be in the tunnel that ends at the door."

"Trevor and Rhys were talking about that Maddox guy coming later tonight," said Llew. "Cover your torch with your hand as much as you can in case we hear him coming."

"You'll hear him before I do," said Jackie. "Your ears are much better than mine."

Llew took Jackie's hand and began leading her down the tunnel. "I wonder what's happening to Gappy and Pru," he murmured. "I hope Trevor and Rhys don't hurt them."

"Me too," Jackie agreed. "Maybe they'll just lock them up. I can't wait to get back home and tell Mom and Dad so we can rescue them."

"Yeah, and those *recruits* they were talking about too," added Llew. "It sounds as if they've kidnapped a bunch of people off the street and locked them up somewhere, ready for some type of ceremony."

Jackie shivered nervously. "The *biting* ceremony. I can just guess what that's gonna be like. We've simply got to rescue them."

They had reached the next fork in the tunnel by now, and Llew guided his sister into the right-hand entrance. "We're going as fast as we can. And what about Mr. Dusk? I couldn't believe it when they said he was here too. I mean, how on earth could he show up just here, in North Wales, of all places."

"I know. Maybe Gappy's a Dusk magnet," Jackie giggled shakily, making a feeble attempt at a joke. "There's something about him that attracts Mr. Dusk, or vice versa."

At last they arrived at the next fork, turned left, and jogged along the last stretch to the wooden door. Llew opened it a crack to take a peek into the tunnel beyond. All was dark and quiet, so they went through the doorway and walked down the tunnel, taking care not to trip on the rough floor or scrape themselves on the wall.

They came to the crate at the end of the tunnel and climbed up onto it. Then Llew, who was the taller of the two, scrambled up through the hole in the roof and put his hand down to pull Jackie up. They quickly made their way to the entrance of the shed, squeezed past the men's car, and darted over to the bushes where they had hidden their bicycles.

Jackie looked sadly at the bike that Gappy and Pru had used. "I really hope they're okay. It feels wrong somehow to be going home and leaving them here."

"I know what you mean," Llew agreed, picking up his bicycle. "We have to, though. Look, do you want to ride your own bike now? It's pretty dark, and I don't think we should use our bike lamps."

"No, I think I'd better ride with you again," Jackie said. "I'll be too slow if I can't see where I'm going properly."

Llew mounted his bicycle, and Jackie settled herself behind him. She put her arms around his waist and rested her head against him. Her brother had a broad, solid back and it felt comforting to lay her cheek against his warmth.

Their progress was a little slow at first because Llew had to pedal uphill. He was not as strong as Gappy was. Eventually they reached the top of the little rise, and the road leveled out. Llew put some more effort into his pedaling then and soon had the bike zooming along the road, his keen vampire eyes keeping a sharp lookout for any sign of Mr. Maddox.

Through the woods they sped, Jackie's long, blonde hair streaming out behind her like a flag. After the stuffiness of the mine, she quite enjoyed the feel of the night air rushing past her. She gave Llew a little squeeze of encouragement as he swayed back and forth, legs pumping hard.

When they finally exited the woods, Llew eased off the pace a little, panting like a steam engine. They soon passed Cade's house, which was all dark, and at last Llew turned into the driveway of Perryelle Cottage.

Jackie leapt off the back of the bicycle. "Oh, no!" she wailed. "Mom and Dad aren't home yet. We'd better try and call Mom's cell phone. Hurry up, Llew."

Llew got off his bike with a tired sigh. "I'm coming, I'm coming. That was hard work, you know. You're jolly heavy."

They went through the back door into the kitchen, and Jackie yanked off her backpack, grabbed the phone off the wall, and quickly punched in the numbers of her mother's cell phone.

The phone crackled a little in her ear and then went dead. No dial tone. Nothing.

She put the phone back on the wall. "The phones are still out. We'll have to go to a neighbor's house and see if theirs is working. Or maybe they'll have a cell phone."

She and Llew decided not to try Cade's house. Winnie was probably not involved in her husband's funny business, but they thought they had better not risk it. They hurried down the street in the other direction to the nearest neighbor's house, but the windows there were all dark as well and no one came to the door. The next house was the same. No one at home.

"Where *is* everyone?" Jackie exclaimed in exasperation. "It's almost eleven o'clock."

"They're probably all still at the fundraiser, making speeches about the village hall needing a new roof," said Llew. He scratched his head. "We should find a house where young children live. There's sure to be someone at home there."

"The people I babysit for live on the other side of the village," said Jackie, "and the closest people to us who have kids are the Prescotts, but they're away on holiday. Hey, what about that house on the corner in the next street? The lights are on. We could try there."

The house she was pointing to was a small, white cottage with roses climbing up the walls. It had a neat, square lawn in front and a verandah on the side, with pretty flower boxes along the railing. A small fountain played by the front path, the water making a faint splashing sound. Llew dropped a penny in as they walked up to the front door.

"For good luck," he said and rang the doorbell.

The door opened rather quickly, and a tall man stood in the opening. He looked vaguely familiar.

"Can I help you?" he asked in a pleasant voice.

"Can we use your phone, sir?" Jackie asked. "We've got kind of an emergency, and our phone isn't working."

"It's rather late," the man answered, "and I'm going out shortly, but . . . of course, come in." He stepped to one side to let them in.

Jackie and Llew walked past him into a shadowy hall.

"The phone's right there," the man said, pointing to a table that stood along the side wall beneath a long mirror. On the other side of the hall was a coat rack and an umbrella stand.

Llew picked up the phone and tried to get a dial tone, but it was no good. The man's phone was dead too.

"Not again!" Jackie wailed as she watched her brother try several more times.

She happened to glance into the long mirror just then and did a sudden double take. Was some of the man's reflection missing?

Then she looked at the reflection of the coat rack on the opposite wall. Hanging on it was a floppy, black hat, a dark blue scarf, and a long, dark blue coat.

Jackie gasped inwardly as a wave of panic washed over her. She could hardly breathe. *Oh, please don't say they belong to that man who came into Maisie's Tea Room to talk to Trevor and Rhys,* she prayed.

She had only caught a quick glimpse of his face at the teashop because he had been all bundled up in his outdoor things, but with a sinking heart she knew it was him – Mr. Maddox. He must be a vampire, then. And he hadn't applied his Reflecto cream very thoroughly that morning because part of his face was missing in the mirror. And the reason he was going out shortly was because he was due at the slate mine to inspect the prisoners.

All these thoughts raced through Jackie's head as she stood frozen, wondering what to do.

Llew was in the middle of asking Mr. Maddox if he had a cell phone they could use, when Jackie suddenly interrupted him mid-sentence.

"Er, it's okay, sir. W-w-we don't need the phone after all," she managed to say through wooden lips that felt stiff with fright. "Come on, Llew. We should leave now."

Lew picked up the phone and tried to get a dial tone.

Llew stared at her as if she were crazy. "But –" he began.

Jackie grabbed his arm. "It's all right, Llew. Really."

She glanced at Mr. Maddox. He was staring at Llew with a slight frown on his face.

"I'm sorry we bothered you," she stammered.

Llew started to protest again as Jackie grabbed his arm. Then Mr. Maddox caught Jackie's eye, and in that split second his eyes suddenly widened in a flash of understanding. He quickly slammed the front door, whipped out a knobbly walking stick from the umbrella stand with one hand, and grabbed Jackie around the neck with the other.

"Hey!" Llew yelled as Jackie was roughly yanked away from him. "What are you doing?"

"You're the snoopy little kids that live near here, aren't you?" the man snarled in a voice quite unlike the pleasant tone he had used to greet them on the doorstep. "My employees told me about you." He glared at Llew. "They didn't tell me you were a vampire though. But there again, they are quite stupid, so they probably didn't notice."

Mr. Maddox brandished the walking stick at Llew while tightening his hold around Jackie's neck. She gave a strangled squeak.

"So, I'm dying to know the nature of this, uh, sudden *emergency*," he drawled. "Do tell."

Llew suddenly sprang at him, but Mr. Maddox merely whacked him with the walking stick and threw him against the wall with a flick of his wrist.

Llew bounced off the wall and landed in a heap on the floor, the wind knocked out of him.

"Who are you?" he wheezed after he managed to catch his breath. "Why are you doing this?"

Mr. Maddox sneered at him, revealing a pair of sharp, pointy fangs that were not filed flat like those of most modern-day vampires.

"Why don't you ask your sister? She seems to know who I am."

"He's Mr. Maddox, Llew," Jackie said in a small voice.

Her brother's eyes widened in shock. "Oh, no!"

Mr. Maddox sneered again. "Oh, yes, though I don't know how you know my name. Well, whatever. What am I going to do with you? I suppose I'll just have to take you with me. Come along, then, and don't try anything, boy. I'm way more powerful than you are. Besides, I'll do something nasty to your dear sister if you do."

He jabbed the walking stick back in the umbrella stand, grabbed a big handful of Jackie's hair close to her head, and pulled her over to where a still-wheezing Llew was getting to his feet. He grabbed the back of Llew's sweater and propelled the children ahead of him down the hall to a small kitchen at the back of the house and through a side door into a garage. Then he hauled them around to the trunk of a car that was parked there and transferred his fistful of Jackie's hair to the hand that was clutching Llew's sweater. Jackie was forced to bend awkwardly sideways with her cheek against Llew's back while Mr. Maddox took a key from his pocket with his free hand and unlocked the trunk. It sprang open, and he ordered Llew to climb inside.

Llew hesitated. He hated the thought of being shut into small spaces. In fact, being shut in the trunk of a car was one of his main fears, ever since he was small and had seen a TV show where the gangster had locked one of his enemies in the trunk of a car in the middle of nowhere and left him for dead.

"Get in," Mr. Maddox growled again, "or I'll twist your sister's ear off."

Jackie squealed as he gave her ear a cruel pinch.

Llew clambered into the trunk and lay curled up with his

back against the back seat. Mr. Maddox made Jackie get in too. When she was settled next to Llew, he gave them a final sneer and slammed the lid of the trunk closed.

They heard him open the car door and shut it again then start up the engine. The car rolled slowly out of the garage, turned right, then left, and rapidly picked up speed as it took off up the road toward the Penffordd Slate Mine.

"Llew, oh, Llew," Jackie kept saying as they were thrown from side to side every time the car hit a bump in the road. "Oh, Llew!"

Llew said nothing to comfort her. He was probably too busy trying to deal with his own claustrophobia.

Luckily the journey to the mine only took five minutes, but to the children locked in the stuffy trunk it seemed like an eternity. At last the car stopped with a jolt, and Mr. Maddox opened the trunk.

"Out!" he commanded.

Jackie and Llew climbed stiffly out of the trunk. Mr. Maddox hustled them over to the shed and made them squeeze past Rhys' car that was still blocking the entrance. He kept threatening to hurt Jackie if Llew tried anything.

He shoved them down the hole in the floor, somehow keeping a firm grip on Jackie's hair all the while. Although this was very painful, Jackie tried to keep her whimpers to herself. She did not want to give Mr. Maddox the satisfaction of knowing how much he was hurting her.

Once they were all down below, Mr. Maddox gave Jackie a flashlight to hold, grabbed hold of Llew's sweater again with his other hand, and marched them both down one tunnel after another. He obviously knew exactly where he was going without need of a map.

After stumbling along the dimly-lit tunnels with Mr. Maddox yanking on her hair whenever she slowed down, Jackie was almost glad when the glow of light from Trevor and Rhys' cave appeared. They passed the rock fall, turned the corner, edged past the fallen slab, and entered the cave.

Trevor and Rhys were sitting at the table playing cards. At the appearance of their boss shoving a couple of children ahead of him, they leapt to their feet in amazement.

"Brought you some prisoners, fellas," Mr. Maddox announced.

"Those are the other two nosey parkers!" Trevor cried. "We've got their mates locked up in the far cell. Where'd you find them?"

Mr. Maddox kept a tight grip on the twins. "They actually came and asked me for help. Said they had some type of emergency and wanted to use the phone. You've got the other two locked up, you say?"

Rhys answered. "Yeah, they came snooping around and we caught them – a boy and a girl. They claimed they were exploring down here alone and the other two weren't with them. We've locked 'em up in their own cell. The boy's a vampire, Mr. Maddox. Knew it right off, I did."

Trevor snorted.

"And the girl?" Mr. Maddox questioned. "Is she a vampire too?"

Rhys nervously twisted his hands back and forth under the tall man's stare. "Well, I could have sworn she wasn't, sir, but apparently she is because she levitated to prove it to us. She didn't want to be separated from her buddy."

Mr. Maddox nodded slowly. "I see. Well, this boy here is a vampire too, but his sister isn't."

"Should we put her in with the other prisoners, then?" Trevor asked.

"No. Lock them up in the far cell with the other kids. I've got to go and inspect the recruits. Watch out for this boy. He's a strong lad. Just threaten to hurt his sister though, and he'll behave." And with that, Mr. Maddox shoved Jackie and Llew at Trevor and Rhys, turned on his heel, and left the cave.

The two men chuckled to each other as they grabbed their flashlights and pushed the children out of the cave. Trevor twisted the back of Llew's sweater so tightly that it almost strangled him, and Rhys got in a few painful yanks on Jackie's hair as he hustled her along. She bit her lip and managed not to cry out.

When they reached the cave where the prisoners were, Jackie and Llew saw a row of people standing silently behind the bars. The prisoners were staring straight ahead with blank looks on their faces while Mr. Maddox stood in front of the bars, peering into the face of one of them – a woman wearing a blue dress. Hanging onto her skirt, with the same blank look on his face, was a little boy of about six or seven years old.

Rhys giggled from behind Jackie. "Handy trick that. Calms 'em right down. Wish I could do that to my wife."

Mr. Maddox turned and glared at them. Rhys snapped his mouth shut and scuttled past with Jackie, but not before giving her hair another sharp twist.

They came to the bend in the tunnel, turned right, and there was the cave cell that held Gappy and Pru.

"Brought some friends of yours," Trevor announced loudly. He took the key off the hook and unlocked the gate. "Stand back and don't try anything, otherwise we'll hurt this pretty young lady here."

Gappy and Pru backed up as Trevor opened the gate and shoved Llew into the cell. Rhys gave Jackie's hair a final twist before he shoved her in too.

Trevor locked the gate and returned the key to the hook.

"Sweet dreams," the men jeered mockingly as they walked away, taking their flashlights with them.

Chapter Fourteen

The Rescue

As the light faded, the four children immediately felt for each other and had a group hug.

"How did they catch you?" Gappy asked. "We thought you'd managed to escape."

"We did," said Jackie, her voice muffled by someone's shoulder in her face. "But when we got back, Mom and Dad weren't home yet, and the phone still didn't work, so we went to the neighbors' house. But they weren't home either because half the village is down at the fundraiser. So then we went to the first house that had lights on, and it just happened to be Mr. Maddox's house – you know, the guy that met Trevor and Rhys in Maisie's Tea Room? – but we didn't recognize him at first, and his phone didn't work either."

She turned to Llew. "Why didn't your vampire radar warn you about him, Llew?"

Llew shrugged. "I don't know. It didn't work that time."

Jackie turned back to the others. "Anyway, then I noticed part of his reflection was missing in the mirror, and then I looked at his hat and coat hanging up in the hall, and I realized it was him. And then somehow he realized I knew who he was, so he slammed the front door and grabbed me and threw Llew against the wall. And then he made us get into the boot, er, trunk of his car and brought us here.

"We saw the people they're keeping prisoner. They just stared at us through the bars like zombies. And Mr. Maddox was there too, staring into their faces, doing his *examination*, or whatever. And they've even got a little boy locked up in there too! And those poor people don't know that in a few days some horrible vampires are going to come and bite their necks and turn them into vampires too, so they can be slaves to a bunch of evil people like . . . like . . . Hillary Sleeth, who sounds perfectly horrid!"

After this long speech had tumbled out of Jackie in one long, seemingly-continuous sentence, she gulped in a deep breath and let it out in a sob. "I thought adventures were supposed to be exciting," she moaned. "But this is just plain scary."

Llew patted her arm. "It'll be okay, Jackie. At least we're all together. We can put our heads together and try to think of a way out of this mess."

He looked at Gappy and Pru. "So what happened to you guys? And how did you make them think you were a vampire, Pru?"

"Oh, they told you that, did they?" Pru felt for Jackie and gave her a quick hug. "It wasn't me, though. You'd better tell them, Gappy."

"Let's sit down first," Gappy suggested.

When they were all sitting cross-legged in a circle, he told Llew and Jackie about the telekinesis and how he had managed to make Pru levitate a few inches into the air so the men would not split them up.

Llew whistled softly when Gappy had finished. "That's cool. I wish *I* could do telekinesis. I can see why you'd have to keep it a secret though. Imagine the possibilities? Breaking into any bank you liked, stealing the Crown Jewels from the Tower of London . . ."

"Yeah, except you're forgetting I can't walk through metal yet," Gappy reminded him. "And soon I'm sure it's going to get harder for me to go into places unless someone invites me in first."

"You've got a point there," Llew nodded. "I'm almost twelve, and I'm just starting to get this funny, tingly feeling sometimes when I go into a building. It makes me kind of catch my step, sort of like a whole-body hiccup. It's probably going to get worse and worse from now on."

Gappy let out a sudden laugh. "Remember how funny it was at Camp Widdershins, when we had to role play ways to get regs to invite us into buildings without knowing they were doing it?"

Jackie gave a little giggle. "Yeah, it was funny watching you do it, too."

"Seriously, though," Pru said. "Just before you arrived, Gappy and I were discussing ways to escape."

Llew and Jackie perked up.

"Go on."

"How?"

Gappy explained. "Well, you and I obviously can't walk through these solid metal bars, Llew. Stone walls I can do, but not more than a foot thick. We're not strong enough to bend the bars, and we can't use telepathy on Trevor and Rhys because they told us their minds have been blocked by the people they work for —

"By the way, Llew, don't let your mental guard down. And you girls should be careful to keep repeating a word to yourself in case Mr. Maddox tries to snoop around inside your heads. That's probably how he kind of recognized you, Jackie. You were probably feeling so anxious that your thoughts were going a mile a minute. Some of them probably escaped into the air, and Mr. Maddox picked up on them."

Jackie and Pru immediately chose a word and started repeating it over and over in the back of their minds. Gappy smiled at Pru. He knew her special word was always her favorite food — *sausages.*

"So, anyway," he continued, "I was thinking I could try and use telekinesis to get that big key to unhook itself and float over here so we can unlock the gate and escape. The only thing is, the key's about ten feet away and I can't see it because of the shape of the wall. I've only been able to move things a few feet so far, and it's always things that I can see. It's worth a shot, though."

"Try it right now, Gappy," Jackie urged at once, but Llew shook his head.

"No, we should wait until Mr. Maddox and Trevor and Rhys have left for the night."

Jackie slumped back against the wall. "You're right. How will we know when they've gone?"

"We might not," said Gappy. "We might just have to wait a while and then risk it."

The time dragged by. Jackie complained that she had left her backpack at home. They could have done with a snack to pass the time. The late hour and the stress were taking their toll on the four children. They tried to make themselves comfortable as best they could, and as they leaned against the back wall of the cave, their heads soon began drooping onto their chests.

Some time later Gappy woke with a start and looked around. The others were still sleeping. What had awakened him? Had Mr. Maddox and his goons left the mine yet? The glow from the lantern by the prisoners' cell did seem to be dimmer than before. Maybe the men had turned it down because they were leaving for the night.

Gappy sat still and listened for a moment, but the only sound he could hear was Llew snoring gently at the end of the row. Even though he would not have been able to hear the men in their own cave, two tunnels away, he had a feeling they were gone.

I might as well have a go at moving that key while the others are sleeping and can't distract me, he thought. *I got a good look at it when Trevor took it off the hook, so I can see it clearly in my mind. Won't they be surprised if I wake them up and dangle the key in front of their faces?*

Gappy got to his feet and went to sit by the bars. He closed his eyes and brought up the picture of the key hanging on the hook. Once he had the image firmly in place, he imagined a beam of energy reaching out from the middle of his forehead, stretching along the wall, and a-a-r-r-round the corner into the little hollow. The edges of the key began to glow in his mind's eye as the energy beam surrounded it. Then he gently nudged the key upwards. Up, up, it went, so slowly and . . . there! It was off the hook!

Gappy tried to steady the key in the air, but it was too late. Gravity took over and the key fell to the floor, landing with a little tinkle of metal on stone.

Gappy muttered a bad word under his breath and glanced at the others, but they were still sound asleep. He could barely see the black key on the floor in the shadows, but he aimed his energy beam at it again. After a few seconds the key suddenly quivered and began to move.

Dragging something by telekinesis was definitely easier than lifting something. Gappy whistled soundlessly between his teeth as he worked on reeling in the key with his mind. It slid steadily along, making a faint scraping noise on the uneven ground. At last, when it got close enough, Gappy reached through the bars and picked it up.

"Voila!" he breathed triumphantly and took a few deep breaths. Why did vampire skills always seem to involve holding your breath, at least when you were first learning them?

Gappy shuffled over to his sleeping companions and shook them. "Wake up, sleepy heads. It's time to go."

Pru sat up and rubbed her eyes. "What time is it?"

*Gappy whistled soundlessly between his teeth
as he worked on reeling in the key with his mind.*

"Just past one-thirty, Wednesday morning," Gappy told her. "And look!"

He brandished the key in her face.

Pru squinted to see what he was holding, then she gasped. "Gappy! You did it!"

Jackie and Llew sat up wide awake at the sound of Pru's loud gasp. They stared in delight at the big key in Gappy's hand.

Llew jumped up and did a few neck rolls. He felt stiff from sitting slumped against the wall. "Wow, great job, Gappy! You managed it! Is it safe to escape now, d'you think?"

"I think so," Gappy said.

"Quick! Unlock the gate!" Jackie squealed.

They crowded around Gappy as he inserted the key into the keyhole and turned it.

Click. The gate swung open. Pru and Jackie clasped hands and jumped up and down in relief.

"I hope this key fits the prisoners' lock too," said Gappy. "I'd really like to rescue them as well."

They went out of the cave, turned left, and walked down the tunnel to the other cave cell. All the prisoners were sleeping huddled together at the back of the cave, except for the mountain man and the woman in the blue dress, who were sitting by the bars talking softly to each other. Their heads jerked up in surprise as the children approached.

"Who are you?"

Gappy fitted the key into their lock and tried to turn it. "We were prisoners like you, but we managed to get hold of the key and escape. Hopefully we can rescue you too."

For a moment the key stuck in the lock, but then it turned all the way, and Gappy pulled the gate open.

The mountain man rushed out. "Freedom! Thank you so much! I don't know why we've all been locked up down here, but thank you for releasing us." He shook hands all around.

"My name's Ted. Who are you?"

Gappy and the others introduced themselves but did not say anything about why they had been locked up. They obviously could not tell Ted that two of them were vampires, or that Ted and his fellow prisoners were being fattened up – or, rather, *healthed* up – like *Hansel and Gretel*, in preparation for the biting ceremony.

The woman in the blue dress was at the back of the cave, shaking the other prisoners awake. "Wake up. It's time to leave. We've been rescued. Wake up."

At the word *rescue*, all the prisoners sat up. And when they saw that the gate to their cell was open, half of them jumped to their feet and rushed out of the cave. The other half hung back looking uncertain and waiting for someone to tell them what to do. They all seemed a little dazed, but maybe they were still feeling the effects of being *examined* by Mr. Maddox.

The woman in the blue dress came out last, leading the little boy. Ted, who seemed more alert than the others, took charge.

"Folks, listen up. We've got to stay together. These kind children have come to rescue us." He looked at Gappy. "Do you know the way out? I think it would be easy to get lost down here. Where are we, anyway?"

"You're in a slate mine in North Wales," Jackie told him. "We've got a map, but we've been here a couple of times now, so we know the way out."

"North Wales!" Ted exclaimed. "Right, you kids take the lead then. We'll follow you." He turned to the other prisoners. "Two by two, okay? It's probably narrow in places. And hold hands so we don't lose people in the dark."

The other prisoners nodded and sorted themselves out. There were ten of them altogether – five women and four men, plus the little boy.

"Should we take the lantern with us?" Jackie asked. "We

don't have any torches."

Llew nodded. "Good idea. And we can get the other lantern from the men's cave too when we go past."

Gappy started off down the tunnel with Jackie, who was holding the lantern. She had turned up the wick so that it burned brighter. For the people at the back, however, it was still quite dark, and this made them move along more slowly than the people in front.

When they reached the cave with the table and chairs, Gappy paused while Ted went in and picked up the lantern off the rocky shelf. The big man spied some matches lying on the card table and lit the lantern, then took his place at the back of the line.

It was a silent little party that wove its way through the tunnels. The rear people could see just as clearly as the front people now, so everyone moved along a lot faster. Past the fallen slab they went, then right, past the rock fall, down the tunnel, left, right, and left again. Everyone hurried as fast as they could, anxious to get out into the open air before the men returned and caught them escaping.

Eventually they reached the wooden door, and each person held it open for the next person to pass through. And so they came to the wooden crate beneath the hole in the roof of the cave.

"It's closed!" said Pru, pointing upwards.

Sure enough, the round concrete cover had been placed back over the hole, blocking the exit.

Chapter Fifteen

Home at Last

Gappy and Llew looked at each other. "I should be able to shift that stone cover if I use my vampire strength," Gappy murmured. "But the prisoners mustn't see."

Just then Ted barged up to the front. "Let me have a go," he said, placing his lantern on top of the crate. Gappy and Llew stood back as he climbed up. The huge, tall man had to bend over to avoid hitting his head on the cave roof. He bent his knees, placed his meaty hands against the round stone cover, and shoved. Grunting with effort, he managed to move it upwards and a little sideways. Then he put his hands against the edge of it and shoved some more until it almost cleared the hole.

"Phew, that was heavy," Ted said. He was panting a little, and his face was bright red. He wiped his sweaty forehead with the back of his arm and stuck his head through the hole to take a look.

The rescued prisoners crowded around the crate. They seemed a little more lively now.

"What do you see?" someone asked.

"What's up there?"

"It's a shed, as far as I can tell," said Ted. He bent down and picked up the lantern, then held it up through the hole.

"Yeah, it's a big shed. There are some tools and mining equipment, and the front's wide open.

"No car?" Jackie asked.

Ted shook his head. "Nope. I'd say it's about time we escaped this joint, wouldn't you? Before the men come back."

The woman in the baggy, grey sweatpants suddenly darted forward and started scrabbling up the side of the crate. "Get me outta here. Get me outta here," she chanted.

The scrawny man tried to shove her out the way in order to climb up himself, stepping on Gappy's foot in the process.

"Hey, watch it," Gappy yelled.

The other prisoners suddenly started pushing each other in a panic to climb the crate.

The sweatpants woman slipped back and trod heavily on Pru's foot.

Pru yelped. "Be careful! You can't all climb up at once, or someone's going to get hurt."

"That's enough!" Llew snapped as loudly as he dared. "Climb up one by one. Gappy and I will help you climb up the crate if you need help, and then Ted can help you through the hole."

He looked up at Ted. "Okay, Ted?"

"Fine," said Ted. "You gotta be calm, folks. Listen to the young fella. We don't want no broken legs or injuries here."

Gappy took over. "Once you're through the hole, make your way outside and around to the left. You'll see some big bushes. We'll all meet up there."

The prisoners muttered amongst themselves, but they all seemed to accept Gappy and Llew as the leaders.

"Jackie and Pru will go first," Gappy continued, pleased that the prisoners were now listening to him. "They'll show you where the bushes are."

He turned to the girls. "Pru, you wait by the door to show them where to go. Jackie, you wait behind the bushes to keep everyone together, all right?"

Jackie and Pru nodded.

"What's your name?" Llew asked the woman in the blue

dress.

"Susie," she answered meekly, still clutching the little boy's hand. "And this is my son, Dafydd."

"Well, after Jackie and Pru have gone up," said Llew, "I think the women should follow, starting with you, Susie, and then Dafydd."

After that everyone calmed down and became a lot more orderly. Jackie and Pru climbed up onto the crate, and Ted hauled them up through the hole in the roof. Pru then stationed herself just inside the shed door to show the prisoners which way to go, and Jackie went to stand by the big bushes to receive the prisoners and keep them together out of sight.

Susie and Dafydd went up next and then the woman in the sweatpants. The other three women and the four men followed, one by one. There was a sense of tense urgency in the air. No one talked now, each person concentrating on the task at hand.

Finally Gappy and Llew climbed up onto the crate and were hauled through the hole by Ted. Then Gappy helped him push the manhole cover back over the hole. Ted looked surprised that it was Gappy helping him and not the burlier Llewellyn. He looked even more surprised at how fast the stone slab was moving. They had it in place in no time.

"You must be a lot stronger than you look," he remarked, wiping his grimy hands on his pants.

The boys and Ted found Jackie and Pru and the other nine prisoners sitting on the ground behind the big clump of bushes.

"What now?" Ted asked.

Gappy spied Jackie's bicycle lying on its side where he had left it earlier. "One of us could go on the bike to get help while the others make their way back to the village on foot, keeping under cover as much as possible."

He looked at Llew. "Your parents are probably home by now, wouldn't you say?"

Llew looked at his watch. "It's about three o'clock in the morning, so I should think so. If they've realized we're not in our beds, they're probably going bonkers wondering where we are."

Jackie gave a huge yawn. "Let's hurry back. I've had enough of this adventure." Her yawn started everyone else yawning too.

"So who's going on the bike?" Gappy asked.

"I think you should," said Pru. "We'll have to keep to the trees on the way back and stay off the road, and Llew and Jackie are less likely to get lost."

"Pru's right," Llew agreed. "You ride back, Gappy, and sound the alarm, and Jackie and I will lead everyone home."

Ted spoke up. "Go on, son. Go get help."

Gappy looked around at the little gathering of people, then he picked up Jackie's bicycle, waved goodbye, and wheeled it over to the road.

"Be careful, Gappy," Pru called after him.

With a final wave, Gappy climbed on the bicycle and began pedaling up the slope.

* * * * * * * * * * * * * *

Llew took charge. "Listen up, everyone. We'll go two by two, like we did before. Jackie, you hold one of the lanterns in front. Ted, you've got the other lantern, so you bring up the rear."

After everyone had sorted themselves out, Llew led them up the slope, keeping to the cover of the trees a few feet back from the road. After a little way he turned left onto a rough trail that led deeper into the woods.

"Where does this path go?" called Pru softly from her place

in the middle.

"It skirts around the pond then comes out in the fields of our farm," Llew called back.

The little procession followed him down the trail, everyone moving as fast as they could by the light of the two lanterns. Even so, people were forever tripping over tree roots and stones in the shadows. It seemed like ages before Llew finally came to a halt at the edge of the woods by a stone wall.

He waited until everyone was gathered around him. "How's everyone doing?"

The men and women quietly indicated that they were doing okay, but a tearful Dafydd piped up that he was thirsty. Susie picked him up. "As soon as we get to safety, you can have a nice big drink of water, okay, dear?"

Dafydd shook his head. "No. I want juice."

Several people laughed.

"My mom's got some juice in our fridge at home," Jackie told the little boy. "When we get back, you can have *two* big glasses, if you want."

"O-o-kay," Dafydd whimpered as his mom set him on his feet again.

"Right," said Llew. "We have to climb over this wall and cross some fields now. We'll be out in the open so we should put the lanterns out. At least there's some moonlight to see by. Just walk slowly and carefully and watch out for the sheep. They'll be scared of you, though, so they should move away when you get close to them. We'll have to climb over a few stiles too."

He looked around at the tired faces. "Everyone ready?"

Everyone nodded yes.

Llew hoisted himself up onto the top of the stone wall and dropped down the other side. The others helped each other over, one by one. Then Llew began to lead them across the field.

* * * * * * * * * * * *

Meanwhile, how had Gappy been getting along? First he had summoned up a little vampire strength to help himself pedal quickly up the slope to the woods, then he had let it fade when he reached the flat part. Now he was wheeling steadily along, keeping a sharp ear out for any sound of an approaching car. As he pedaled, he went over the night's happenings in his head.

I'm so glad we were able to rescue the prisoners. That biting ceremony sounded horrible. I can imagine if I was one of the prisoners and that creepy Mr. Dusk bent over me to bite my neck. Yuck!

Let's see. There were ten prisoners, and three vampires were coming to do the biting. So they were probably going to bite three people each. What about the tenth one, though? Maybe they weren't going to bite Dafydd 'cause he's just a little kid. Or maybe they were each going to take turns biting him. It takes three bites to change someone into a proper vampire — or at least that's how it works in the movies. Mom and Dad won't talk to me about that sort of stuff, so I dunno.

By this time Gappy had come to the end of the woods and was pedaling down the open road. He sped by Cade's house. A dim light glowed in one of the windows, and Rhys' old brown car was parked outside. He finally reached the driveway of Perryelle Cottage and turned into it with a thankful sigh. The house looked dark, and Uncle Peregrine's station wagon was poking out of the garage, so his aunt and uncle were home.

Hoping the kitchen door was still open, Gappy pedaled around the side of the house. *They must not have realized we're missing,* he thought. *Just went to bed, I guess.*

He leapt off the bicycle and laid it on the ground. Then he started toward the kitchen door and —

"— Oof!"

Someone had come up behind him, grabbed him around

the waist with one beefy arm, and clapped a large hand over his mouth. Gappy promptly kicked the person in the shin, but although the person gasped in pain, he merely tightened his grip around Gappy's waist and began dragging him towards the kitchen door.

"Mmmm, mmm!" Gappy mumbled, muffled by the big hand over his mouth. He summoned up some vampire strength to try and break free, but the person holding him was much stronger. Gappy was dragged, kicking and mmmming, through the kitchen door and thrown on the floor. Instantly a light snapped on, and someone gave a loud gasp.

"Gappy! Thank goodness!"

Gappy sat up and looked around. Uncle Peregrine and Aunt Joelle were sitting at the kitchen table looking at him with worried expressions on their faces. Standing by the wall, his hand on the light switch, was a dark-haired man wearing a formal suit and tie. A tall woman with short, windswept black curls, dressed in jodhpurs, riding boots, and a cream-colored sweater, lounged against the draining board. She was smacking the side of one of her boots with a short whip and smelled of horses.

The person who had nabbed Gappy outside and dragged him in was revealed to be a short, burly-looking man wearing jeans and a blue tee shirt with a picture of the Rolling Stones on the front of it.

"Good work, Gary," the smartly-dressed man told him in a deep voice.

Gary nodded at the compliment. "I'll go back to my post then." He looked down at Gappy. "Sorry 'bout that, mate. You put up a good fight, though." And with that, he went outside, closing the door behind him.

Uncle Peregrine helped Gappy to his feet.

"Who are you?" Gappy asked the two strangers.

"We're from the Vampire Council," the man answered. "I'm Lord Ballantine, and this is Cecily – "

"Gappy, where have you been?" Aunt Joelle interrupted. "Where are the others?"

"Yes, do you realize what time it is?" demanded Uncle Peregrine. "Gone three-thirty in the morning! We've been looking all over for you since we got home and found you weren't in your beds. Your aunt was all set to call the police, but of course we had to call the Council first in case your disappearance was vampire-related."

"Perry, Joelle," Lord Ballantine broke in, "give the boy a chance to speak. Sit down, son, and tell us what's going on."

Uncle Peregrine pulled out a chair next to Aunt Joelle, and Gappy sat down on it with a grateful sigh.

His aunt put her arms around him and hugged him. "I'm so happy to see you, Gappy. We've been so worried."

Gappy let her hug him then jumped to his feet again. "We've got to go find the others."

Lord Ballantine laid a hand on Gappy's shoulder. "I think you should tell us what's going on first."

"But –"

Lord Ballantine gently pushed Gappy down onto his chair. "Quickly now."

The woman in jodhpurs stuck out a shiny, black boot and hooked out a chair from under the table. She turned the chair around and sat on it backwards, leaning her crossed arms on the back of it.

"Yes, do tell," she drawled. "I've been called away from a riding party for this, so it had better be good."

"Sissy!" exclaimed Lord Ballantine in an irritated voice.

"Okay, but can I have some water first," Gappy croaked. His throat felt parched from bicycling home so quickly.

Lord Ballantine filled a glass of water from the tap and

handed it to Gappy. The boy took a few gulps then set the glass down.

"It all started when we saw this man called Rhys driving away from the Penffordd Slate Mine," he began.

As Gappy quickly told his tale, his aunt and uncle listened intently. They could not help gasping when they heard about Trevor and Rhys discussing what was going to happen to the homeless prisoners and that Mr. Dusk had reared his ugly head again, all the way across the Atlantic.

Aunt Joelle gave a little moan when she heard about her children being shut in the trunk of Mr. Maddox's car and locked up in the mine as well. She leapt to her feet. "Gappy's right. What's everyone waiting for? We've gotta go rescue them!"

"It's all right, Aunt Joelle," said Gappy. He told her about getting the key and rescuing all the prisoners, who at this moment were making their way to Perryelle Cottage, led by Llew and Jackie.

His aunt sat down again with a huge sigh of relief and felt in her pocket for a tissue. "That's good," she said tearfully. "Very good. Oh, Gappy." She broke into a fit of sniffs and blew her nose hard. Uncle Peregrine put his arm around his wife and patted her back.

Lord Ballantine stood up, the pinstripes of his suit making him appear taller than he was. "Which way do you think Llew will be leading the prisoners, Perry?"

"He said he was going to stay away from the road," Gappy put in.

"They're probably coming across the fields then," said Uncle Peregrine, his arm still around Aunt Joelle.

"Right," said Lord Ballantine. "Sissy, you and Gary go out and see if you can find them."

Without a word, Sissy flowed off of her chair and stalked

out of the kitchen to find Gary.

Lord Ballantine turned to Gappy. "So you say this Maddox person lives near here?"

"Yes," Gappy answered. "I'm not sure which house it is, though. Llew and Jackie will be able to tell you when they get here. I don't know if he'll be at home now, but we know he'll be meeting up with Mr. Dusk and the others at Harlech Castle on Friday night."

Lord Ballantine looked thoughtful. "Hmm, that's in three days. We'd better get cracking. This is going to need some planning. We'll have to nab Trevor and Rhys first, of course, before they can give the game away, and then we'll try to round up Seymour Dusk and the others when they're all together, if not before. Hmm, Hillary Sleeth . . . we've had our eye on her for some time."

Gappy laid his head down on the table. "I hope Llew and the others get here soon. I'm tired."

"Why don't you go and have a quick wash and put your pajamas on?" his aunt suggested. "I'm really cross with you, Gappy, for getting into danger and exploring places you had no right to be, but I'm very proud of you as well."

She clasped her nephew's hands. "My children are safe because of you. *Thank* you, Gappy."

Uncle Peregrine added his thanks too, accompanied by a hearty clap on the back, and Lord Ballantine told Gappy he was proud to have met him.

"Fine young man, yes indeed," he muttered as he took his cell phone out of his pocket. "A fine young man." Then he began making the first of several urgent calls to important people in the London branch of the Vampire Council.

Chapter Sixteen

A Shocking Chill

Gappy went upstairs to freshen up. He felt drained after all the night's excitement, and he was hot and sweaty from his fast bike ride. After a quick wash he put on his pajamas and went back downstairs. As he entered the kitchen, Aunt Joelle handed him a mug of tea. It was warm, milky, and sweet, and tasted delicious.

While everyone waited for Llew and the others to arrive, Lord Ballantine asked Gappy some more questions about his adventures. He and Uncle Peregrine were most interested to hear how Gappy had learned to do telekinesis at such a young age, especially since he had managed to make it appear that Pru could levitate.

Finally, after what seemed like an eternity of waiting, a commotion was heard outside. The kitchen door opened and Sissy stalked in, followed by a bedraggled-looking Jackie and an equally tired-looking Llewellyn and Pru.

Aunt Joelle leapt out of her chair and rushed over to them. "Oh, oh," she murmured as she hugged them all long and hard. "I'm so glad you're safe. Gappy's been telling us all about it."

She eyed the weary procession of people filing in through the kitchen door and reluctantly loosened her grip on the children.

"Come this way," she said, waving the rescued prisoners through to the living room. "I'll put on a kettle for tea. Make that *two* kettles," she added as more and more people crammed into her kitchen.

Ted brought up the rear, carrying Dafydd in his arms. He smiled at Gappy. "All right, son?"

Gappy grinned and threw him a salute.

Uncle Peregrine went to get everyone settled while Lord Ballantine debriefed the twins and Pru in the kitchen. They were joined by the snooty-looking Sissy, and Llew warily eyed the whip that she laid down on the table in front of him.

"She was at a riding party," Gappy explained, then helped his aunt with the tea trays while he listened to Llew describing how he had led his procession of escapees home. They had met up with Sissy and Gary in the middle of a field.

The sun was coming up when Lord Ballantine finally took his leave after thanking Gappy and the others again for all their hard work. With an approving whack of her whip on a shiny boot, even Cecily whatever-her-name-was admitted that the four children had done *rather* well but should be careful not to let their heads get too big over it.

With a last goodbye, Gappy and the others trudged upstairs to bed. They fell asleep almost as soon as their heads hit their pillows.

* * * * * * * * * * * * *

It was just after midday when their hungry stomachs woke them up. Drawn by the delicious smell of breakfast cooking, they wandered downstairs and found Aunt Joelle in the kitchen putting an egg-and-bacon casserole on the table, accompanied by a spring green salad and thick slices of crusty French bread slathered in butter.

"Fabulicious!" Llew murmured in approval, his mouth watering.

Uncle Peregrine came in just then. "Ah, brunch. Good, I'm famished. All this excitement, you know . . ."

"*We're* the ones who had the excitement, Dad," said Llew.

"Yes, well, all the worry, then," his father said, sitting down and helping himself to a slice of French bread. "You really gave us a scare, you know."

"Did you call my mom and dad?" Gappy asked, feeling a little worried at what his parents' reaction would be.

Uncle Peregrine nodded. "Yes, we called both of them. I spoke to them first, and then Lord Ballantine spoke to them. Your mother was shocked and cross about it, Gappy. She said to tell you to consider yourself grounded for a whole six weeks when you get back, for breaking your promise. What promise was that, might I ask?"

"Oh, just that I wouldn't be getting into any more adventures," Gappy mumbled around a mouthful of egg.

"It wasn't Gappy's fault, though, Dad," Jackie put in gamely. "Llew and I wanted to have the adventure, and Gappy came along to protect us."

Pru nodded and took a huge bite of French bread. "S'true . . . sort of. You didn't call *my* parents, did you?"

"No. There's no reason to worry them," answered Aunt Joelle, laying her hand on Pru's shoulder for a second. "They don't know anything about vampires, do they? It would be too difficult to try and explain things to them."

"What happened after we went to bed, Uncle?" asked Gappy with a smile at Jackie for sticking up for him.

Uncle Peregrine ladled some more egg-and-bacon casserole onto his plate. "Well, some hefty members of the London Council's cleanup crew flew over this morning and paid Trevor a visit. Rhys was there too. They're both locked up now in the reg section of Grimlock Vampire Prison on the Isle of White."

"Good name for a prison," Aunt Joelle laughed rather shakily as she handed her husband a cup of tea.

He took a sip. "I suppose it is. Anyway, apparently Trevor and Rhys both went crazy when they were arrested. Kept asking if they were still going to get bitten so they could live forever. I guess Maddox had promised them that if they did their jobs well, especially controlling the prisoners during the biting ceremony, the last few bites would be reserved for them."

"Ugghh!" Pru shivered at the thought. "We never did see the cave where the biting ceremony was supposed to be held, but I can just picture it – a gloomy, dungeony-type of place with water dripping everywhere and heavy chains bolted into the walls to lock up the prisoners – "

"– and evil vampires looming over them," Llew continued, "with long, sharp fangs and blood dripping down their chins from the last victim they just bit, and – "

"Ooh, stop!" squealed Jackie. "I don't like thinking of vampires that way. You and dad are vampires, and you'd never do that."

"Yes, I'd also rather not think about the dark side of vampirism, if you don't mind," Aunt Joelle agreed, with a little shiver of her own.

In an unconscious reflex, Gappy had begun rubbing his tongue over his filed-down eye teeth. He caught sight of Llew doing the same thing, and they smiled a little awkwardly at each other across the table.

"What about Cade and his mother, Winnie?" asked Jackie. "And where did Ted and all the homeless people go?"

"Mrs. Paskin was asleep in bed when Trevor and Rhys were arrested," said Uncle Peregrine. "She didn't know anything about what her husband was up to. In fact, she seemed rather relieved when it was explained to her that he'd gotten into trouble and has to disappear for a long time. She's planning to move to Scotland to live with her sister. There's a good school there for special children like Cade, and it has a rather fine music program too.

"The homeless people have all been bussed to the Council's country estate near London where they will stay for a while. They'll never know the real reason they were kidnapped, of course, and they will be well looked after.

"As for that nasty Mr. Maddox, unfortunately he wasn't home, so the plan is to capture him and the others when they meet up at Harlech Castle tomorrow night. Meanwhile, the cleanup crew will stake out Maddox's house and the Pennfordd Slate Mine in case he shows up beforehand. I only hope he doesn't get suspicious when he can't get in touch with Trevor and Rhys."

Gappy sat back in his chair. He felt much better with a full stomach. "Everything seems to have been sorted out, then. I really hope they catch Hillary Sleeth and Diggory Humbold and Mr. Maddox – boy, what a mouthful – and especially Mr. Dusk. I'm sick of him turning up wherever I go."

"Yes, why did they just happen to choose *our* little village?" Llew asked. "It's such a coincidence."

"I've been wondering that myself," said his father, nodding. "I think maybe they felt drawn here because this little corner of North Wales has quite a long history of vampirism. As you know, Tristan Glyndwr came from here, and there are quite a few sacred vampire spots in this neck of the woods, besides the stone circle at Creigiau Gwyrgam that your great-great-grandfather liked so much."

Aunt Joelle put some vampire vitamins and iron pills in front of Gappy and Llew and poured them each a glass of calves' blood to swallow them down with. "If you don't mind, and to save my sanity, will you please all promise me that you won't go looking for any more adventures when you meet up at Camp Widdershins this summer?"

"Aw, Mom," began Llew, but changed his mind when he caught sight of his father's stern eye.

"I promise," he said, but he crossed his fingers under the

table as he did so.

Gappy and the girls promised too, although Gappy had a feeling that he might find it a difficult promise to keep. Danger just seemed to follow him around lately.

* * * * * * * * * * * * *

The next three days were taken up by trips to the beach and a horse ride at a nearby stable, but everyone was waiting on tenterhooks for Friday night to hear if the Harlech Castle raid had been a success. Lord Ballantine had promised to call them as soon as it was over.

Friday night finally arrived, and Aunt Joelle and Uncle Peregrine did not even attempt to tell the children to go to bed. They all sat in the living room, drinking mugs of tea and wondering how the raid was going.

It was almost midnight when Lord Ballantine called Aunt Joelle's cell phone to tell them that Hillary Sleeth, Diggory Humbold, Raymond Maddox, and Seymour Dusk had all been captured by the vampire cleanup crew. They were now safely in custody, headed for Grimlock Prison on the Isle of White.

Gappy let out a huge sigh of relief as his aunt began collecting up the tea mugs. He felt he could relax at last.

"Rrrrring!" went the house phone.

"Oh, good, the lines are fixed," said Aunt Joelle as she backed out the door with her tea tray, "though who else would be calling at this time of night, I don't know. Answer it, will you, Gappy? You're the closest."

Gappy walked over to the phone and picked up the receiver with his left hand. "Hello?" he said.

There was no answer, but he thought he could hear the faint sound of someone breathing softly on the other end.

"Hello?" he said again.

The soft breathing continued.

"Prank," Gappy mouthed to the others, who were all looking at him. He was just about to replace the receiver when . . .

". . . aaaaaaahhhhh," a wispy, far-away voice sighed into his ear.

An eerie, cold feeling suddenly sprang up in Gappy's left hand and began creeping up his arm.

"It's the oh-so-clever Gustavus Grapple, isn't it?" the faint voice continued. "It's time to come home, Gustavus. I want you. Come home. Come home.

"C-o-m-e h-o-o-o-o-ome."

The fading voice ended in a muffled chuckle. Then there came a distant click, followed by dead air.

Gappy slowly replaced the receiver, stumbled over to the nearest chair, and sat down heavily on it, as if the stuffing had been ripped out of him. The cold feeling was now creeping all over his body, and he felt suddenly nauseous.

"What is it, Gappy?" Pru exclaimed, rushing over to him. "You've gone all white. Who was that on the phone?"

Gappy raised his head, a look of anguish on his face.

"I don't know," he whispered. "I thought it was the Master at first, but now I think it was someone else. Someone more evil."

He shivered and wrapped his arms around his cold body.

"He told me he wants me.

"He told me to come home."

The End

Welsh Pronunciation Guide

Abergath – AB-air-GATH

Beddgelert – Beth-GE-lert (dd is like the th in teethe)

bore da – borra DAH

Clogwyn – CLOG-win

Cwm Hetia – Coom HET-ya

Creigiau Gwyrgam – CRY-gyeye GWEER-gam

Cymru – KUM-ree

Dafydd – DAV-eethe (like teethe)

Dilys – DILL-iss

Dinorwig – Deen-OR-wig

Dyffryn Ardudwy – DUH-frin Ar-DEE-dwee

Glyndwr – Glin-DOO-er

Harlech – HAR-legh

Llanafon – Sthlan-AH-von
(ll does not have an equivalent in English, but sthl is close.)

Llanberis – Sthlan-BEH-riss

Llanfairpwll – Sthlan-VIRE-poossl

Llyn Dinas – Sthlin DEE-nas

Llyn Gwynant – Sthlin GWEE-nant

Penffordd – PEN-forth

Rhys – Reece

Sygun – SUH-geen

Look for Book Six of the
Young Vampire Adventures:
Gappy and the Witch's Curse

Visit Gappy at
www.gappy.tv

or search for Gappy
on Facebook.

Acknowledgments

My deepest thanks go to Robert J. Jones, Associate Professor of Foreign Language and Humanities at Fulton-Montgomery Community College, who very graciously advised me on Welsh translation and pronunciation. The fictitious villages of Abergath and Llanafon owe their names to him.

Thanks also to my readers, Emmalee Hoppe and Ella Brownson, who enthusiastically edited the manuscript with red pen and offered suggestions from a young person's viewpoint. They both told me I had to explain what a priest hole is.

Briony Allan heard the plot first and came up with the title of this book, and elementary school teacher, Anthea Morris, was as invaluable as ever in the editing process.

And finally, thanks to my friends, Dr. Scott Bello, for answering last-minute questions about the effects of autism and spina bifida on violin-playing, and Professor Curt Breneman for advice on safety catches and guns.

Author's Note

All of the places named in this book are real, except for the villages of Abergath and Llanafon and the stone circle, Creigiau Gwyrgam. Harlech Castle was built in 1283-1290 for King Edward I, and as far as the world of regular humans is concerned, it has only one dungeon beneath the north-west tower, which was accessible through a trapdoor.

www.ingramcontent.com/pod-product-compliance
Lightning Source LLC
Chambersburg PA
CBHW022216050726
47590CB00002B/819